The Last Layover

The New Homefront, Volume 1

By Steven C. Bird

The Last Layover: The New Homefront, Volume 1

Copyright 2014 by Steven C. Bird

Written and published by Steven C. Bird at Homefront Books

Edited by Sara Jones at www.torchbeareredits.com

Illustrated by Keri Knutson at www.alchemybookcovers.com

Print Edition (6.18.15)

ISBN-13: 978-1507808573

ISBN-10: 1507808577

www.homefrontbooks.com

www.facebook.com/homefrontbooks

scbird@homefrontbooks.com

Table of Contents

Disclaimer

The characters and events in this book are fictitious. Any similarities to real events or persons, past or present, living or dead, is purely coincidental and are not intended by the author. Although this book is based on real places and some real events, it is a work of fiction for entertainment purposes only. None of the activities in this book are intended to replace legal activities and your own good judgment.

Some items in this book have been changed from their actual likenesses to avoid any accidental sharing of Sensitive Security Information (SSI). The replacement values serve the same narrative purpose without exposing any potential SSI.

Dedication

To my loving wife and children:

Monica, Seth, Olivia, and Sophia

You inspire me to be a better man. It is my constant desire to protect you and provide for you that drives my imagination in ways that allowed me to create this story to share with others. Every day that I wake up, I hope that I can use that day to somehow improve myself so that I can be a better husband and father. Hopefully, this book, a result of the inspiration that you have given me will help me do just that. I love you all.

Introduction

The winds of change had been sweeping through America for some time now. Certain political factions controlling the mainstream media had been working toward their goal of redefining the nation into their own image of government-centered collectivism. Through the media, public schools, and a near fascist use of political correctness, they had been changing the opinions of the uninformed public and the way they see traditional American values.

A constant assault on religious faith, as well as chipping away at America's pride in its history, work ethic, and rugged individualism, had the left country divided. To those who paid attention, this division seemed hopeless to repair. Add to that, out-of-control government spending and political leaders who seemed intent on collapsing America's economy with burdensome social programs and business-killing regulation, and it's understandable why so many constitutional and libertarian-minded Americans had become uneasy about the future.

Survivalists and doomsday preppers who were once on the fringe had now been joined by a low-key wave of mainstream conservative and libertarian Americans. Cable TV shows depicting prepping, as well as myriad websites and both fiction and non-fiction books had proliferated, feeding this hunger for answers in an insecure world.

Americans from all walks of life had begun preparing for the uncertainty ahead. One of the more prevalent fears was the almost certain coming collapse of the house of cards on which the nation's economic security was based. Whether this fragile situation had been brought on intentionally to be able to rebuild America into a new form after the collapse, or unintentionally by inept politicians who sold their oath of office to any special interest group that would bankroll their careers, one thing was sure; it just could not go on like this forever.

Evan Baird, a captain with a large regional airline, closely followed the events that unfolded in America as a result of this insidious agenda. Evan retired from the Navy Reserve at the age of forty. Soon after, he and his wife, Molly, purchased their dream home, an older brick farmhouse on one hundred acres in the beautiful mountains of East Tennessee. They began turning their little piece of Tennessee heaven into a hobby farm which soon became their passion in life. They had longed for a peaceful country lifestyle to raise their family for quite some time, which would also help them to be able to provide for themselves in the event the country began to unravel.

Chapter 1: The Alliance

As like-minded individuals seem to coalesce around one another, Evan and a coworker, Jason Jones, became good friends and allies. Jason was a pilot with Evan's company. Like Evan, he was based in Columbus, Ohio, at the Port of Columbus International Airport. Evan was a captain and Jason a first officer aboard their company's Embraer 170, 175, and 190 family of aircraft. As coworkers in two different, but closely-knit positions, the men were afforded ample opportunities to fly together as a crew.

Jason was an Army Infantry veteran in his late thirties with a wife and two young sons. He had the unique ability to be hardcore, direct, to the point, and humorous all at the same time. Jason and Evan shared the same constitutional libertarian ideology, loyalties, fears and concerns. They also shared the same desire to protect their families, above all else, making them a natural alliance. They discussed ideas and strategies and even trained together when able, keeping each other on track mentally and physically.

Although Jason and Evan were diligent in their preparations and training, one major roadblock existed that they did not know how to adequately mitigate. Their job as domestic airline pilots kept them away from home on average, two weeks or more per month. Traveling by air limited their abilities to take along bug-out bags, as most people who traveled to work by car or truck could. A pilot typically carried only three bags for an overnight trip. One was a flight case, which was a rectangular case, usually made of leather or heavy nylon. The flight case was used to carry charts and manuals that were legally required for flight operations, as well as a few items such as a flashlight, batteries, and an aviation headset. There were not many options for utilizing this bag any further, as it was already packed to its capacity with the required items. Their main suitcase was a carry on sized roll-aboard containing clothes and hygiene items. The third bag was a cooler-type lunch bag. Both

Evan and Jason had one additional item in this bag: a Sig Sauer P229, chambered for the .40 Smith & Wesson cartridge.

After the terrorist attacks of September 11, 2001, Congress authorized the establishment of the Federal Flight Deck Officer (FFDO) program. The FFDO program was implemented as part of the Department of Homeland Security and the U.S. Air Marshal Service, allowing trained pilots to carry firearms. Being defensive-minded individuals and prior military, both Evan and Jason attended the training at their own expense in their off time and became deputized as FFDO's.

This program was a huge benefit for Evan and Jason; it allowed them to feel as if they continued to serve their fellow Americans after leaving the military. It also gave them an advantage if they were away from home working if—or when—a SHTF (Shit Hits the Fan) event occurred. This was the only way a traveling pilot could take a weapon on the road. The TSA security screening at every airport would prevent them from even having nail clippers, much less a firearm.

Traveling crewmembers regularly swap planes and are often reassigned to different flights, so checking a bag was simply not an option. In parts of the country where the second amendment was severely restricted, like Chicago and New York, the federal status of the FFDO program trumped state and local law. This allowed them to always have their duty weapons in their possession at their hotels during their overnight layovers. Each of them also carried an extra box of fifty rounds of duty ammo along with their official duty load out of their issued magazines. They knew the loaded magazines alone, though more than adequate for the intended purpose of the program, would not get them very far if things took an ugly turn after some sort of event.

Jason lived just a little more than an hour away from Columbus, in Zanesville, Ohio. Evan, however, had to commute to work by flying out of the Tri-Cities Airport in Bristol, Tennessee, or the McGhee Tyson Airport in Knoxville. Once at work, their schedules often consisted of mostly four-day trips that kept them on the road—figuratively speaking—on overnight layovers in company-provided hotels in a different city each night.

As of late, the country had been in an almost daily decline. The current administration had been pushing more and more expensive social programs on the country, in what appeared to be an attempt to intentionally break the back of the economy through debt and taxes. In what had become a quarterly debate on raising the already staggering national debt ceiling, the president immediately cut off food stamps and other government entitlement programs. He blamed the opposing party, and various constitutional and libertarian-minded groups who champion smaller government, due to their resistance to the increasing debt. This divided the country even further, causing small riots and acts of violence all across the country. It was a nation at a tipping point and seemed that, any day, the country would plunge into a state of emergency. All it needed was the right nudge.

Feeling the inevitable, Evan and Jason started bidding for trips at work together. When they got schedules with other crews, they did whatever they could to swap and trade around with other pilots in an effort to line their trips up as best as possible. Knowing that their family's security plans depended on the two of them making it back, they were determined to strengthen the odds by working together as much as possible.

They both started packing their roll-aboard luggage accordingly, as well. It was October, and cooler weather had begun to prevail in many parts of the country that they frequented. They had discussed the best way to pack for work and to bug out at the same time. Their uniforms, which were made like business suits with the associated dress shoes, would not be of much use to them in a survival situation. Since they had limited space to pack, they decided that casual looking hiking boots would fit the bill for footwear. They could be worn with regular clothes and not look out of place. Also, in the event of having to stomp sod for any extended period of time trekking home, they would be a godsend for their comfort and protective qualities.

Casual-looking, tactical cargo pants, a few short sleeve shirts, some long sleeve shirts, and a zip-up fleece jacket with a removable outer shell, would round out their functional clothing requirements. Choosing all natural, earthy colors like tans, greens, and browns would allow them to blend in with the natural environment if need be while also serving as daily wear. In addition, they each bought a cheap, thin backpack, such as one a high school kid would use; those were flattened and packed empty into their roll-aboard suitcase. This would serve as a bug-out bag in the event one was required, as dragging a wheeled suitcase around would not be practical in a survival scenario.

Each of them also packed tortillas, flat packets of tuna, chicken, and some instant coffee singles. These items took up very little space in their roll-aboard but would give them a couple days' worth of emergency food. They also carried iodine tablets, a water filter survival straw, ibuprofen, a stainless camping mug, antibacterial ointment, an assortment of bandages, and a cigarette lighter. They felt these basic items would get them going in the right direction. Additional supplies could be acquired along the way if need be.

The most important preparation they felt they needed to make was to be able to establish communications with their families. If a catastrophic event occurred and they still had cellular service, landlines, and internet connectivity, then keeping in contact with both homes would be easy. However, considering the state of the union and similar events elsewhere in recent history, one would have to assume that the government may use the opportunity to declare martial law. In such a case, communications could be taken offline or strictly controlled and monitored "for the safety of the people." Control of information is always one of the first steps all dictatorial governments or regimes take when making their final push for control. However, even in the absence of nefarious domestic or foreign government intentions, those technological communication mediums that we now rely so heavily on would not exist at all with the failure or destruction of all or part of the country's fragile power grid resulting from a natural or man-made disaster.

To address their communication contingency strategy, Evan and Jason decided to utilize contacts they had acquired through work and like-minded preparedness organizations. Both the Baird and Jones households had HAM radio stations, and all of the adult family members were trained in their basic operation. Evan and Jason used their human contact network to develop a series of friendly and trusted HAM operators located near their likely layover points and potential routes of travel. These contacts would be included in their route plan in order to coordinate with the Baird and Jones households until they made it safely home.

Both families understood that if an event occurred while Evan and Jason were away, to listen on a prearranged frequency "on the nines," at nine in the morning and then again at nine at night. Once initial contact had been made, this frequency could be adjusted to fit the given conditions.

Chapter 2: Flight 4225

It was the end of October. Evan and Jason were starting a four-day trip together the next morning. Evan had to commute to Columbus the night before, as the trip had an early report time. He called Jason on his way to Knoxville to catch a flight. When Jason answered the phone, Evan asked, "Got your gear packed?" This was a question he already knew the answer to since Jason was a bit more on the "all business" side than himself.

Jason just responded sharply, "You know it! I'm ready for the zombies."

"Screw the zombies; they would be harmless compared to the city rats."

"Very true; so why don't you just spend the night here? We've got room."

"Thanks, but I've already got a hotel room booked," Evan replied. "Besides, you need your family time. We can catch up during the trip. Just pick me up at the hotel tomorrow morning on your way."

"Roger that, Boss. Are you staying at that dump again?"

"Yep, the Skyway Lodge. Yes, it's a dump, but it's cheap. That leaves me more money for beans, bullets, and Band-Aids. Besides, I was in the Navy, so I have low standards for my accommodations," Evan answered.

They shared a laugh, said their goodbyes, and went on with their respective evening plans. Evan spent the night at the hotel in Columbus. After tucking his kids in bed over the phone, he told his wife he loved her. She was getting increasingly nervous about his travel, given the state of things. No matter where she looked, every television channel, newspaper, and internet news source contained reminders of how the fabric of society was unraveling. The only difference was who they blamed. He felt the same; he just didn't let it show. If given a choice, he would have gladly changed careers so he could remain closer to home. Unfortunately, with a record unemployment rate and the seemingly daily occurrence of local businesses shutting down—or relocating out of the country—there were simply no opportunities to be had. This was the hand that he had been dealt, so he had to play it.

Early the next morning, Jason picked Evan up right on time, as always, and they headed for the airport, stopping briefly at a Dunkin Doughnuts drive-through window. Evan often referred to coffee as his life support system. Flying long hours on an ever-changing schedule with commuting thrown into the mix will wear one down over time.

Once they reached the airport, they met up with their two flight attendants, Glen Brooks, and Peggy Marshal. Glen had been with the company for several years and was a fun, entertaining guy to have along. He lived in Boston, and like Evan, commuted to Columbus for work. Always cracking jokes with a twisted and unabashed sense of humor, he kept things lively.

Peggy was a new hire just out of initial training. At twenty-six years old, she was eager to start a new life for herself after a painful divorce. She was a single mother with a five-year-old son named Zack. Her parents were comfortably retired and lived just across the river from Cincinnati in Newport, Kentucky. They graciously volunteered to watch her son while she was away for work. They knew she needed this change in her life, so they were willing to accommodate her in any way they could. This was only her second real trip flying the line after her completion of training. She felt a mixture of nervousness and excitement about her next four days on the road. Since she lived in Cincinnati, she drove to Columbus early that morning and arrived ready and raring to go. Evan and Jason enjoyed working with new hires as they usually had a positive attitude. They found this refreshing since the airline industry tended to leave people bitter and jaded, given enough time.

The economy became so bad, people were not flying as much as they had in the past. Businesses cut back their travel significantly in order to cope with the changing economic climate; the average leisure traveler and vacationing family simply could not afford to travel like they once could. This was further impacted by the fact that the current administration had cut funding in areas that would intentionally inflict pain on the American people. This was done to garner support for the president's ever-increasing deficit spending. Unfortunately, air traffic control had been one of those cuts. With fewer controllers on the job, airlines did not have the departure and arrival slots they used to have in the congested traffic of the northeast.

"Today is a total waste of a day of my life," as Evan put it. "Only one flight to JFK and we're done for the day, stuck in that place," Evan said this aloud; he did not hide the fact that he didn't have much love for densely populated urban areas. The corrupt and oppressive governments, overcrowded everything, and voter bases that kept the wannabe dictators in power left a bad taste in his mouth.

Jason just sighed in agreement as Glen quipped back, "Stuck here? I love New York. I'm going clubbing tonight if you rednecks wanna go."

"No thanks; all I brought to wear was my camouflaged NRA shirt, and I doubt they would let me in wearing that," said Jason.

"Damn straight! You gun nuts just keep to your Tea Party rallies and Klan meetings and leave the clubs to the rest of us," Glen said, jokingly.

"Deal! Except for the Klan part, of course. You do realize your side founded the KKK, right?" Evan replied. "Besides, you'll come crying to us gun nuts for help when the zombies come."

"Hell no! My ass will get eaten right away. I wouldn't last five minutes in a zombie apocalypse. I've watched The Dead Walking or whatever it's called. You can keep that world," replied Glen in an intentionally snarky manner.

They all shared a laugh, then got on with their respective duties. Although Glen, Evan, and Jason did not see eye-to-eye on political or social issues, or much of anything else for that matter, they had a mutual respect for each other and enjoyed working together while giving each other a hard time.

Flight 4225 got off a few minutes late due to late arriving passenger baggage but was otherwise uneventful. The cool fall morning air provided them with nice smooth rides, helping the flight attendants complete their in-flight beverage service with ease. During the cruise portion of the flight, Evan and Jason caught each other up on the goings on in their lives while Glen took rookie Peggy under his wing and helped her with her duties in the back. The weather going into New York was crystal clear. It was one of those beautiful mornings without a single bump in the sky. The cool morning air was as smooth as glass, the winds were calm, and the temperature/dew point spread gave them near unrestricted visibility.

As they were being vectored up the Jersey Shore toward JFK by air traffic control, they could see all of Manhattan Island and Long Island. Jason turned to Evan and said, "Man... that's the last place I want to be when shit hits the fan."

"Ditto," Evan responded. "Just imagine being down in the middle of that mess when things go down. It would be just like the Will Smith movie *I Am Legend*, when people were fighting to get off of the island, trampling women and children for the last helicopter or ferry. Oh, and, of course, the city rats would be in heaven amidst the lawlessness. That just makes me glad we are pack'n."

"Hell, yeah," said Jason. "That, and you would have a long way to go to get away from it all, even if you were lucky enough to get out of NYC itself. The traffic would be total gridlock, and that's if the roads were even open at all. On top of that, the urban sprawl just seems to go on forever, so humping it out on foot wouldn't be a picnic either."

As they made their final approach to the airport, Evan looked at Jason who was flying this leg and said, "You'd better grease this one because after that smooth ride, the passengers will definitely notice if you bonk it. No pressure, though," he said with a devious smile.

Jason just replied, "Oh, ye of little faith." He then added a few knots of airspeed to their calculated final approach speed and said, "That's for a cushion."

Evan looked at him and said, "Just don't float it. A greaser that touches down beyond the touchdown zone doesn't count as a good landing, no matter what the passengers think."

Jason chuckled. "Watch and learn, brother," he said as he brought the airplane in for a landing so smooth it was hard to tell if they had even touched down.

As they rolled down the runway and decelerated with the thrust reversers, Evan said, "Well, you set the bar high for my next one with that."

"I do what I can to keep you on your game, old man." The two always had some sort of healthy competition going on between them.

With the reduced flights and such, it seemed eerily quiet as they taxied to the gate. What not too long ago was a bustling, congested airport was now ghostly quiet with just a few aircraft taxiing around. On the bright side, Evan thought, at least there wouldn't be lines trying to get in and out of this place like before. The U.S. economy was so depressed, at least twenty percent of the domestic flights had been removed from the regular schedule. The Middle Eastern, Asian, and European airlines seemed like they were still running at normal capacity, however.

"Those foreign airlines don't seem to have cut back any," Evan commented, taking notice.

"Yeah, they must be coming here for the cheap shopping now that the dollar is so weak, just like how Americans used to feel in Mexico with the peso," added Jason. They just nodded in agreement with mutual disappointment for the current state of the country and the world.

Upon reaching the terminal, Evan pulled the aircraft into the gate. As what seemed to be common practice these days, they had to wait for about fifteen minutes for a gate agent to arrive to operate the jet-way. Once she arrived, she pulled the jet-way up to the main cabin door and the passengers were deplaned. The crew gathered their things, secured the airplane, and headed out of the terminal for their extended layover in New York.

With the JFK airport being located on Long Island, just east of Manhattan, the crews always stayed at the Rockville Center Suites Hotel near Rockville Center on Long Island. The hotel was conveniently located just two train stops away from Madison Square Garden in Manhattan. There were a few local pubs and restaurants and a nearby train station, but otherwise it was mostly a retail and residential area. It was close enough to the hustle and bustle of downtown that crews on overnight layovers could easily visit while also being far enough away to be able to avoid it.

The crew made their way through the terminal to the curb for their ground transportation to the hotel. Once they were on their way via the hotel shuttle van, Glen said, "Hey, I'm hitting the train station and spending the day in the city, and tonight who knows what? Who's with me?"

Being new to the whole scene and excited to explore, Peggy said, "I'm in, but I'm flat broke so I can't spend much."

First-year flight attendant pay is basically poverty wages, and with the company deducting the cost of their uniforms from their first paycheck, they were not left with much. The first few months on the job for flight attendants without someone to help support them is usually a ramen-noodle-every-meal kind of lifestyle.

Glen said, "Don't sweat the money, honey, it will be a blast and I'll help you out. Besides, you're a cute young thing; plenty of guys will be willing to buy your drinks where we are going. How about you two rednecks? Are you still gonna slam-click me?"

Slam-clicking is a commonly used phrase to describe a fellow crew member who simply slams their hotel room door and clicks the lock, not to be seen again till the next day. A slam-clicker is essentially a stick in the mud.

Evan laughed and said, "We can't keep up with you young'uns all night. You two have fun."

"Suit yourselves," replied Glen as he redirected his attention to his smartphone.

For the next few miles, the crew sat quietly and watched the city go by through the van's tinted windows. As they passed by a local grocery store on the way to the hotel, Jason noticed a crowd and some commotion going on out front. A police patrol car appeared to have arrived at the scene only moments before. The officer seemed to have his hands full and backup had yet to arrive. Jason asked the van driver, "What the heck is going on there?"

The van driver said, "Oh, those damn right wingers and tea baggers won't help the president and have shut the government down again! Because of them, he can't pay for the food stamps these people depend on to get by. Those fools have got to go! These people get their food stamps cut off and are desperate, so they just take the food. The store calls the cops then the next thing ya know we got a mini riot."

Evan and Jason just sat there, biting their tongues. They knew they couldn't accomplish anything discussing the issue in the last few miles to the hotel, so there was no point even attempting to make the argument. It seemed to them that over half of the population was no longer capable of objective critical thought, allowing the corrupt to use the ignorance of the masses as a powerful political weapon. As Thomas Jefferson said, "If a nation expects to remain ignorant and free, it wants what never was and will never be."

Chapter 3: The Layover

When the van finally arrived at the hotel, they gathered their bags and proceeded inside to the lobby to check in. While checking in, Peggy said, "Sorry, Glen, but I'm broke so I'm gonna have to pass. Maybe next time."

Glen looked disappointed but determined. "Your loss, sugar. Have fun with those two rednecks there." He smiled at Evan and Jason, relishing in the opportunity to take a stab at them in fun. They chuckled, rolled their eyes, and let it go.

After checking in, Evan, Jason, and Peggy got into the elevator while Glen chatted up the hotel front desk clerk. As soon as the door closed Peggy said, "Thank God you guys are staying. After seeing that mob scene at the grocery store a few miles back, I changed my mind in a hurry. I don't want to be out in this place and have something like that happen."

Evan said, "Well, we are walking a block down the street to a little Irish pub for a bite and a beer later. You're welcome to join us."

"Yeah, their bangers and mash are the best," added Jason.

"Sure," she said. "What time?"

"How about six?" Jason queried.

"Works for me! I'll see you guys then," she said with a smile.

The elevator arrived at their floor, and they each went their separate ways. Once in their rooms, they made their phone calls home to let their loved ones know that they had made it safely to their hotel. They changed clothes and made their way downstairs at six o'clock to meet for dinner. On the way down, Evan and Peggy bumped into each other at the elevator. Peggy was still on the phone, chatting with her mother, so Evan checked his social media on his phone while the elevator took them to the lobby level.

Upon arriving in the lobby, Peggy wrapped up her call. There stood Jason, tapping on his watch with a stern face. "You are late!

Beer o'clock was three minutes ago. Happy hour is burning!"

"Yeah, yeah, we'll do better next time, sir," Evan said with a smirk.

After a short walk, they arrived at the pub and grabbed the last available table, near the main entrance door. They arrived just as it was getting busy with the after-work crowd. Evan and Jason were both comfortable and warm in their hiking boots, cargo pants, and jackets; however, Peggy wasn't quite as appropriately dressed. She wore slip on sandals, yoga pants, and a light jacket. She complained about the cold every time the door opened as patrons came in and out. Evan and Jason just nodded and smiled at her frustrations. Once the waitress arrived, Evan ordered his favorite India Pale Ale, Jason his standard order of a dark and creamy Stout, and Peggy a typical American light beer. They both snickered at her order, being self-described beer aficionados, and then offered up a toast.

"Here's to another day flying and not making the news," Jason said. As they raised their glasses, they felt a tremble through the ground, then heard a muffled *thump, thump, thump* off in the distance. This was followed almost immediately by the lights going dark.

There were a few drunken cheers in the pub by patrons expecting the lights to simply come right back on; however, they did not. It was nearly seven o'clock in the evening and, being late October, it was already dark outside. Evan went over to the door and looked around to see that all of the buildings, except for a random few that must have had emergency generators, were dark, as well as all of the street lights. Traffic immediately started to back up as the traffic signals were no longer functioning. The situation was only made worse by drivers who stopped to look around, trying to figure out what was going on.

He quickly walked back to the table and told Jason and Peggy, "Time to go!"

Jason immediately stood up and grabbed his coat, seeing the seriousness on Evan's face. Peggy just sat there looking at the two of them like they were crazy and said, "What? Why? We haven't even started on our beer yet. The lights will come back on in a minute."

As Evan placed a twenty dollar bill on the table to cover their drinks, he said, "I'm afraid not; the entire city is out. Remember the grocery store? Do you want to be in the middle of something like that in the dark?"

She immediately grabbed her purse and they walked out the door while all the other pub patrons stood around, confused and waiting for the lights to come back on. They made their way back to the hotel, walking at a brisk pace down the dark sidewalk. Evan and Jason both wished they had their handguns with them instead of having them out of reach in their rooms at the hotel. The sidewalks were getting more crowded by the moment as people came out of the darkened buildings to find out what was going on. Just like most of the people standing around on the sidewalks, Evan, Jason, and Peggy were all checking their phones, trying to find a signal. To their dismay, it appeared that no one had service in the area, regardless of the provider.

As they approached the hotel, they heard another series of booms in the distance. "That doesn't sound like transformers exploding," said Evan with a concerned voice. "It's too muffled, almost like it's coming from underground, like at a mine or construction zone."

When they reached the front of the hotel, they were relieved to find that it at least had its emergency lighting on. The automatic doors were not working, so they entered through the side entrance that someone had propped open.

Once inside, they stopped to talk to the front desk clerk to see what he knew. He said he had no idea what was going on, but explained that they had a backup generator. Unfortunately, it was only enough to power the lobby, hallway, and stairwell emergency lighting systems. He said it was there for insurance reasons. Otherwise, the miserly owners would not have sprung for it.

He handed them each a ChemLight to use in their rooms and said with a chuckle, "Enjoy your stay with us."

They all laughed, then Evan and Jason shared with him what they had seen and heard during their walk back to the hotel.

"It's never gone out like that before," he said. "Usually, it's a street by street or block by block kind of thing. Oh well, they will get it figured out soon."

Evan and Jason, however, did not share his optimism. Evan, Jason, and Peggy walked over and took a seat in the lobby. They sat there quietly for a moment, soaking in the night's events.

After a few moments of silence, Evan spoke up and said, "Okay, here's what I think. We don't have a clue what's going on yet, but it doesn't look good. After the first couple of booms we heard, everything went dark. The entire city is affected from what we can see, and that's not normal. To top it off, none of our phones work, the desk clerk said the land lines are down, and who knows what those last few thuds we heard were. I say we hunker down for the night and give Glen a chance to make it back. We can formulate a bug-out plan in the morning based on what we learn between now and then, unless, of course, this all turns out to be less than we think."

Jason nodded in agreement as Peggy nervously interjected, "What do you mean less than what we think? What do we think? And what do you mean *bug out*? We can't leave while we are here for work! I'm new and on probation. I'll get fired and I have a child to support!" she said as her voice began to get more excited.

"Calm down, Peggy. Just relax and I'll explain," Evan said. He proceeded to go over all of the changes that he and Jason had been studiously watching the country go through. He explained how the country's economic instability, combined with a government that seemed hell-bent on dividing its own people into favored groups of victims while pitting them against demonized groups of their opposition, made the country ripe for some sort of event to push it over the edge.

"It's textbook, really, if you look at history on how to collapse a country from the outside, using surrogates to do your dirty work, or from the inside via some sort of false flag event. Some of the president's own associates from Columbia University, who are devout Marxists, actually published a strategy on how to do just that in America.

"Just look at the intermittent cutting off of food stamps and benefits that have caused people to snap, like at the grocery store. It's almost as if they have been testing the people to see if they were ripe for the picking. If they will riot over food stamps, what do you think the result would be if you took away their running water, sewage, electricity, cell phone, etc.? They've been trained and conditioned to feel as if they are entitled to what you have, so when you take away their steady stream of government handouts, they will feel justified in taking what's yours."

"But why in the world would people in our own government do such a thing?" exclaimed Peggy.

"Loyalty to the cause—" Evan was interrupted by a loud *POP, POP, POP* that sounded like gunfire coming from just the next street over.

Peggy looked toward the door, her nervousness was apparent. "What was that?"

"The rats are coming out to play already," answered Evan.

"Well, folks, we have to get ourselves in order here," interrupted Jason. "Let's all go back to our rooms for the night. Make sure you deadbolt and flip-latch the door also. Peggy, you need to figure out what is in your suitcase that you really need. Consider things like comfy shoes, warm clothes, medication etc., and put it in your smaller RON bag. Just take your company manuals and put them in your big suitcase along with everything else that isn't critical. If this all turns out to be no big deal, then fine, but if we wake up tomorrow to a different world, we are gonna need to travel light and leave that stuff behind. Let's all meet in my room at 0700 and we will gather any new intel and hammer out a plan."

"Sounds good to me," said Evan.

"Okay," Peggy reluctantly replied.

"Oh, and don't leave your room tonight. Bad people are gonna start taking advantage of the lights-and-phones-out situation very soon; if those shots we heard are any indication, they already have."

Evan and Jason escorted Peggy to her room and waited in the hall until she was safely inside with the door locked and latched. As they walked down the hall toward their own rooms, Jason said, "So what do you think is going on?"

"Exactly what we expected to happen," Evan said. "Every country in the world has leadership that puts the security and needs of their country first. They have built and strengthened their infrastructure, defense, and economic standing. We, on the other hand, have had a government as of late, that seems to do nothing but cash out our value and try and bring us down to everyone else's level, all in the name of appeasement, political correctness, and tolerance. It was only a matter of time before someone took advantage of our self-inflicted situation. Is it Islamic extremists? Is it China or Russia? Or is it from within? Who knows at this point? All I know is, I don't have a good feeling right now."

On that note, Evan and Jason went to their rooms and prepared for what may come. That night, none of the three slept very well, each of them worrying about what might be going on in the world. They worried about how their families were doing back home. Was this event really that widespread, or was it isolated to New York City? Were their families watching all of this unfold on television in complete safety while worrying about them, or where they caught up in the situation themselves? How was Glen? Was he safe? Did he make it back? Will he? Will they have to leave without him?

As all of these unanswered questions swirled around in their heads, their sleep was also interrupted by the occasional sounds of yelling, gunshots, and sirens outside the hotel. Some seemed distant, but others were disturbingly close. Evan and Jason both feared that as the outages carried on, the less-than-desirable elements of society would begin to take more and more advantage of the situation.

After a night that seemed to go on for days, the sun finally came up and the violent noises faded. The three met at Jason's room at 0700 as they had agreed the previous night. Jason and Evan had both pulled their emergency backpacks from their roll-aboard luggage and packed their pre-planned bug-out bags accordingly. They each also had their duty pistols with them and planned to keep it that way for the time being.

As instructed, Peggy replaced the set of company manuals in her RON bag with some casual clothes and a few snack bars that she had packed. A RON bag is the smaller of the two bags that a flight attendant generally carries, with the roll-aboard luggage being the larger of the two. The RON bag typically contains the required items for the performance of his or her duties; however, Jason and Evan felt it would also serve well as a bug-out bag. Its shoulder strap and smaller size would make it fill in nicely for a backpack.

"So, Peggy, what kind of clothes and stuff did you bring with you that may be useful?" asked Evan.

"Well," she said, "I have a pair of yoga type stretch pants, some sweat pants, running shoes, a sweatshirt, a long sleeve blouse, some underwear, socks, four snack bars, and my flashlight that I'm required to carry in my RON bag for work. Oh, and my uniform trench coat."

As Evan and Jason pondered the items she had just listed, they realized that there wasn't much that she had brought with her for durable wear. At least she would be comfortable for extended travel, and several of the items could be doubled up for layered warmth if need be, they thought. The most useful thing she had with her would likely be her uniform trench coat, which could be beneficial for the potential cold nights ahead. It was also of a fairly rugged design which would offer her a certain level of protection if things got rough compared to the rest of her clothes. Jason suggested that they also each take one of the extra blankets from the hotel room closets and stuff them in their bags. *Better to take them now and carry the bulk than to freeze to death later*, he thought.

After their inventory, Peggy said, "So has anyone heard from Glen?"

Evan replied, "I checked his room on the way down the hall and knocked on the door, but there was no answer. I think I should go down to the front desk and see if they've seen him or if they have any news. You two hang tight. I'll take the stairs down and go see what I can find out."

With that, Evan left the room with his Sig Sauer under his jacket. He and Jason would now be defying the draconian New York gun laws as well as their own Standard Operating Procedures (SOP) about off duty, off airport carry. Although both men prided themselves on being law-abiding citizens, they refused to die for the sake of a rule or law, which under the circumstances, did not seem at all relevant. They always joked that when it came to survival, they'd *rather be judged by twelve than carried by six*, as the saying goes. This had definitely become one of those situations.

Evan made his way down the emergency stairwell, and, luckily, it was still being lit by the emergency generator. Once he reached the lobby, he saw that there were numerous people surrounding the front desk demanding answers as if somehow the clerk was responsible for or could actually do something about the situation. He also noticed that it was the same fellow who was on duty the previous evening; he looked worn out and tired.

The clerk, tired of all the yelling and interrupting, climbed up on the lobby counter and yelled, "Listen up people! A police officer came by and told me that there has been a series of what appear to be terror attacks. He said they are not sure of the full extent of it or if it's all over. For now, they are ordering everyone to shelter in place. For us, that means the hotel.

"The emergency lighting, however, only has another day—maybe a day and a half—of fuel, and we can't get more because the gas stations are without power or already out of fuel because people made a run on them as soon as it went down. I guess Hurricane Sandy's post-storm fuel shortages have people paranoid or something. Anyway, given what he said, my dayshift relief isn't here yet, and if he doesn't show soon, I'm leaving anyway. I have my own family to get to. Most of the rest of the day shift staff, for that matter, haven't shown up either. Just a few people who live within walking distance, but there isn't much they can do, so I'm sending them home to their families.

"We are going to pull the complimentary breakfast pastries, bagels, and fruit out for you to hand out. Unfortunately, the boiled eggs, milk, and the other perishables are likely already spoiled because the refrigerators aren't on the generator and have been without power since yesterday. Good luck, I'm sorry I can't do more." He stepped down from the counter and did his best to ignore the eruption of emotion from the crowd as he disappeared back to the office.

A mixture of emotions filled the room. Some people were outraged and continued to seem to want to make demands on the hotel staff. Others broke down in tears or just stood there as if in disbelief. As one of the hotel employees carted out the remainder of the breakfast food, people began to just take what they wanted and stuffed their pockets and bags. Evan managed to get his hands on a few pastries and muffins before it turned into a total brawl.

He noticed another man in his mid-fifties with a calm demeanor looking on in disgust as well. They made eye contact and walked over to each other as Evan said, "My how quickly the weak crumble."

The other man said, "My thoughts exactly. Just imagine how they are gonna behave after a few days without society holding their hands."

Evan stuck out his hand and said, "Evan Baird; pleased to meet you."

"Damon Rutherford," he replied. "Let's take a walk."

The two men left the lobby for one of the adjacent conference rooms. Damon explained that he was an electrical engineer who was in town attending a company conference for the week. They each shared a little information about themselves, both being careful not to give away too much to someone who five minutes ago, was a total stranger but just enough to let each other know they could perhaps be beneficial to each other. Evan told him about his crew and that they were waiting on Glen, who had gone over to Manhattan.

Damon responded, "If he went to the island you're not gonna see him very soon. This morning I went for a walk to gather intel just before coming back into the lobby to witness this mess. I met an EMT, who said the Island was hit hard. By whom, they didn't know. He thought he heard another first responder mention jihadists over the radio, but city officials are throwing around the words *Tea Party* and *right-wing extremists*, but he said that's bull. Not sure why they are messing around saying stuff like that during an emergency, but it's all crap.

"He said they have also pretty much declared martial law and no one is allowed in or out. If you're not a government official, you're seen as a bad guy. Several buildings have been destroyed by bombings, as well as ferry terminals, subways, and even a few nightclubs and restaurants. If I heard him right, even Times Square was hit pretty hard. So if your friend is okay and still there, he's gonna be there for a while."

Evan just looked at the ground for a moment and said, "Well, in light of all of that, I need to talk to my crew; if he doesn't show up soon, I think we are gonna have to move on before this place implodes."

"Oh, and, by the way, you say you're airline?" questioned Damon with a not so pleasant expression.

"Yes, why?" Evan enquired.

"Well," he said, "from what the EMT told me, LaGuardia and Kennedy were both hit and are said to be down for an indefinite time. So my guess is that you're on your own."

"Really? How were they hit? With what?" Evan responded.

"Not sure. It was a quick conversation and he was just giving me a short debrief of what he had seen and heard. If you guys decide to head out, let me know. Maybe we can work together, at least until we get out of the city. I've got a plan, and I'll let you in on it if you decide to go. Let's meet back down here at five o'clock to see if your man made it back from Manhattan and go from there."

"Sounds like a plan," Evan said. "Hey wait, what floor are you on?"

"Ninth," Damon answered.

"Well, we are on the eleventh; let's meet in the stairwell on the tenth-floor landing. That'll save a lot of stairs."

"Sounds good to me, my old knees miss the elevator," Damon replied.

With that being said, both men agreed with a handshake and parted ways. When Evan got back to Jason's room, he explained everything he had seen, heard and learned downstairs. He gave them the pastries that he had acquired before the hotel staff abandoned their posts and said, "For food, this is it. Even with what we have in our bags, we don't have much to hold out on for long. The stores that haven't been looted already can't process any transactions because everything is automated, and face it, because of our own addiction to the grid with our habit of using debit cards instead of cash while traveling, we don't have much to work with. I've got twenty-three dollars in cash left."

"Eighteen for me," added Jason.

"Sorry, but I've only got some loose change," said Peggy in an embarrassed manner.

"That's forty-one bucks and change between us," Evan said adding it up quickly in his head. "That won't get us far, but in reality, paper money is probably not much use right now anyway."

"So what about Glen?" asked Peggy, who seemed more overwhelmed with each passing moment. "We can't just leave him here!"

"We aren't leaving him here; he left us," said Jason as he stood up and walked to the window. He stared out at the view below. "We all have families back home that need us. Your son needs you, our wives and families need us. From what we know now, things aren't getting any better around here anytime soon and who knows what's going on out there where they are. We didn't make Glen go off on his own, and we have no possible way to find him, or to know where he is, or if he's even alive. Besides, he is from Boston, so he may just try and head off that way and we would never even know it. I made an oath to my wife and you have a God-given obligation to your son to make it back to him."

Evan spoke up and added, "Right now the streets are semi-safe during the daylight, but as we all heard last night, after dark the scum have taken over. They know with the power out, there are no security cameras to record their mayhem, and the blackout of streetlights gives them the perfect cover. It won't be long before they realize things have changed for the long term, and then they will be just as bold during the daylight too. If we are gonna get out of this urban nightmare before everything completely falls apart, we have to get moving. Damon's offer may be a good way to go."

"You're right," she said, "but we don't even know what his plan is, do we?"

"That's just good OPSEC, and I think he is showing wise judgment by not sharing the details until he knows who is on his team," Evan said.

"OPSEC?" she queried.

"Oh yeah, Operational Security. It's keeping your plans, resources, strengths, and weaknesses low-key so that others can't use the information to their advantage if they mean you harm."

Peggy nodded in agreement. "Oh, that makes sense."

With that, the three silently agreed to get moving. Deep inside, they all hoped Glen was okay and that he would show up before they left, but there was a hollow, empty feeling that it wouldn't be the case.

As five o'clock approached, Evan, Jason, and Peggy went down to the tenth-floor landing of the stairwell. Damon arrived right on time. He and Evan shook hands with a smile and Evan introduced everyone. After exchanging pleasantries, Damon said, "I'm sorry your friend didn't make it back, but I'm glad to have you all on board. I've got a way out of here, but I'd rather not have to do it alone. I'm no spring chicken. With a knee that's been blown out more than once, I'm entering uncharted waters trying to make it on foot. I'd much rather have a team than be a loner."

"So, where are we going?" asked Evan.

"Well, my brother Jim has an older forty-three foot Viking Yacht, from the late '80s I believe. It's down at the Rockaway Point Yacht Club down by Breezy Point. He lives in Delaware, but he had a guy out of there doing some post-Hurricane Sandy repair work on the canvas top over the flybridge and the rear deck. Whether it's finished or not, it's in running condition and, considering the state of things, he'd be happy if we got it back home to him. It has two strong, running Detroit Diesels and all the gear we need to get it underway. You three help me get to it, get it going, and ride shotgun for me along the way, and once we get to the Delaware Bay I'll take you as far as I can. I should be able to drop you off south of Philly. It's a straight shot over to Ohio from there."

"Ride shotgun?" Evan said with a raised eyebrow. "How did you know we were armed?"

"You're armed?" Damon questioned with a smile. "Well heck, that's even better. I thought we'd be unarmed till we got to the boat. That's a bonus. Knowing my brother, I was just assuming he had something stashed like he usually does."

Evan and Jason glanced at each other with a mutually satisfied look and a nod. Jason then turned to Damon and said, "So how do we get to the boat?"

"Well, it's gonna be dark soon, so I think we should get a good nap in and head out first thing in the morning. That will give your friend a little more time to make it back, if he *is* coming back. Our route, as I see it at this point, is about sixteen miles give or take for deviations as necessary. It basically follows the POW/MIA Memorial Highway to Broadway. We would then follow that to Central Avenue. We will take that west to Mott Avenue, where we will jog north to Channel Beach Drive. We will then take Channel Beach Drive down to Riis Landing. Once we get there, we can get off of the roads completely and follow the beach on down to the boat.

This, of course, is all subject to change based on the conditions we find. I also figure we will need to handrail this route, for threat avoidance reasons, when need be."

"Handrail?" Peggy said inquisitively.

"Handrail is a tactical term for following a route parallel, but off to the side. If you don't want to get ambushed or detected, you don't just walk down the middle of the street," replied Jason.

"Oh, okay," she said. "That makes sense."

Damon then finished by saying, "Well, that's the plan as I see it for now, but I'm sure it will change as soon as we start walking. Sixteen miles would take us six hours in a best case scenario, so we had better plan on all day."

At this point, Evan said, "Okay guys, we are a team now, so let's act like it from here on. Jason and I have rooms next to each other with an adjoining door. Let's all move into those rooms with the door open. That's four beds, and if last night was any preview, I expect it to get worse so being together only makes sense."

Everyone agreed and went to gather their things. They then went back up to the eleventh floor. As Peggy walked down the hall to her room to gather her things, a man approached her and said in a demanding and disrespectful voice, "Hey, how much food do you have?"

"Just a little, why?" she replied nervously.

"Give us what you have. We are collecting all of the food in the building. It will then be handed back out accordingly."

At that time, Evan heard what was going on and walked quickly toward Peggy's room. He looked at the man with a scowl and said, "She's not giving you anything. You've got no right to demand what others have, so just move along."

"Look, buddy," he replied while pointing his finger at Evan in an aggressive manner. "This ain't over. I'm gonna tell the others, and you will give it up."

"You had better just keep way from us. It will be the biggest mistake you've ever made if you try to take anything against our will—that I promise you," Evan replied as he squared off against the man.

"Yeah, whatever, tough guy. I won't be alone when I come back," the man said, walking away, mumbling profanities under his breath.

Peggy looked at Evan and said, "Can't we just give them something so they leave us alone?"

"No way!" replied Evan. "In an emergency situation like this, food is life. Chances are, the reason they are trying to take everyone's food is because they've already scouted around outside and found out there isn't any to be had. A city this size can't feed itself with its lack of production and extreme population density. They need constant resupply from the outside to keep food on the shelves. Give it a few more days, and people will be getting desperate for food and will do anything to get it. That's why we have to get moving and out of this urban nightmare."

A look of hopelessness came over Peggy's face, and she responded with a defeated sounding sigh. This was all a lot for her to bear. She was one of those people who saw modern society with all of its abundance as always being there and could never imagine a situation such as this.

When Evan and Peggy got back to the adjoining rooms, they told the others what had happened. "Freakin great!" exclaimed Jason. "We're not even out of the hotel and we're already getting into it with people."

Just then, another series of *thump, thump, thump* could be heard off in the distance, followed by a loud boom that made the building shutter so that it sounded like it was across the street. Damon ran to the window and saw what appeared to be a car fire one block over. He said, "What, are we in Baghdad? Do we have to deal with IEDs now? Is that what all those booms we heard were? Cars blowing up everywhere?"

Jason joined him at the window and said, "It's almost like a coordinated attack. They started with power generation and transportation. Now we're seeing stuff more locally focused. If you think about it, a grid down scenario like this would give someone up to no good the perfect cover. Law enforcement agencies are overwhelmed, security cameras are down, and no cell or land line coverage to make any reports."

Just then, a UH-60 Blackhawk helicopter flew overhead from the east to the west. Damon pointed at the helicopter and said, "That thing didn't even seem to stop and check out the car fire. That sort of says something about the big picture. Think about it. We've not seen one news helicopter, not one commercial aircraft of any kind, and really no police presence to speak of. Things must be a lot worse than we think, or things are so widespread and serious, that our plight here is small potatoes."

"Hey, guys," Peggy said from the restroom. "The sewage is backing up in here. This is gross."

"Well, hell," Damon said, "either the city sewage system has been hit too or some pumps are down. Does the water still run?"

"No, it's out too," she said.

"Well they, whoever they are, have managed to hit everything," added Damon.

"The streets seem a lot emptier now than before," said Evan, looking out the window. "People are probably catching on that this isn't a simple temporary power outage anymore. And where are all the cars?"

Jason interrupted and said, "Okay guys, uh, and gal, let's hit the sack; we have a big day tomorrow. I think the situation warrants a constant watch now. We have about six hours until we need to get up and on the move. Let's split this night up into three two-hour shifts. I'll take the first, then Evan, and lastly Damon, you can be the early riser."

"Roger that," Evan and Damon both replied.

Things were pretty uneventful during Jason's watch. He heard a few screams off in the distance that gave him the chills. In the pitch darkness of the moonless night, he couldn't see anything out the window. It was eerie how dark a major city could be without power.

The hotel's generators must have finally run out of fuel; the emergency lights had gone out as well. A few gunshots could be heard on occasion. He could only imagine the fun the scumbags were having. This was like a golden opportunity for them. If the police weren't responding to car bombs, then who would possibly care about rape, murder, and robbery?

At the end of Jason's shift, he awoke Evan for his relief. He debriefed him on what he had heard, and Evan took his place on the chair by the window with his SIG .40 holstered up and ready to go. About a half hour into his watch, just as Jason had fallen asleep, he heard multiple footsteps that sounded like they were making their way down the hall. He crept over to the door to try to get a peek through the peephole. As he leaned his head up to the door—*BAM!* The door was kicked open, striking him on the forehead and knocking him backward onto the floor.

Jason, who was barely asleep, awoke to see Evan sitting up on the floor with his gun pointed in the direction of the door. *POP! POP! POP!* Evan fired three shots into the doorway while screaming, "Get out! Get out! Get out!"

A large man fell out into the hallway as the others in the group scurried down the hall to escape Evan's rage. Jason jumped to his feet, grabbed his gun, and covered the door while he ran over to help Evan up. Evan said, "I'm fine, I'm fine. Damon, watch Peggy while we secure the room."

Jason and Evan, both with their flashlights in their non-shooting hand, cleared the doorway and checked the hall. Calling on their previous military experiences and their personal training, they were both tactically proficient and worked well together as a team. They both were active tactical shooting competitors as well, which helped to keep them on their game.

As Jason covered the hallway, Evan looked the downed man over with his light and said, "This is the jerk that confronted Peggy earlier in front of her room, wanting to take her food."

"He wasn't kidding about coming back with more people," replied Jason.

"Yeah, and being in New York, where people don't have the right to own a weapon unless you're a government official, they must have just assumed we were unarmed and thought they could roll over us with brute thuggery," added Evan.

"Well, they know better now," Jason said with a smug grin on his face.

Each of the men shared an uneasy laugh and went back inside the room. Peggy was in the corner huddled up in a ball, shaking and crying. Damon tried to console her. After a few moments, she regained her composure and said, "I can't believe you shot him! All he wanted was food. We should have just given it to him." She struggled to keep from breaking back down into tears.

Damon said to her, "Now, Peggy, Evan did what he had to do. At this stage of the game, an attempt to take your food is an attempt to take your life. It's that simple. Anyone who is gonna bust down your door and rush into your room in the middle of the night plans on doing whatever they have to do to you to get what they want. Do you think they would have attacked us then started playing nice? They decided to take our group out to support theirs, and that's just not gonna happen if we have a say in it."

Jason walked over to her and added, "And chances are, you are going to see a lot more violence before we make it home. Just remember, we are not just fighting to save ourselves, but to get home to our families to help them through this ordeal as well. And not one thug out there deserves consideration at the expense of your little boy."

"You're right, guys. I'm sorry, Evan."

Evan smiled at her. "It's okay."

Damon stood up and said, "Alright, folks, it's time to regroup. Let's go into the other adjoining room where we at least have a door still on its hinges and figure everything out."

Once in the other room, with the adjoining and main doors locked, they pulled the recliner in front of one door and pushed the dresser in front of the other.

"That will at least keep them from kicking another door into Evan's head," said Jason with a smirk.

"Ha ha," Evan replied.

Damon stood up and walked over to the window. "I think we need to get underway sooner than we had planned. We can use the dark as cover to slip out of the hotel without being obvious to our fan club downstairs. It won't be long until the sun is up, anyway. How do you guys want to handle this?"

Jason said, "I think we should use the fire escape. I'd rather avoid going down eleven flights of stairs, with each landing being a kill zone from the associated floor hallway. Plus, these jokers are probably focused on the inside of the building and more than likely don't have a sentry on each corner of the building exterior. Evan, you provide cover while I climb down, then we can both cover Damon and Peggy from top and bottom since they're unarmed. Once they are safely on the ground, you follow while I cover you."

"Sounds like a plan," Evan said in agreement.

"Now, everyone grab your stuff and put your extra layers on because it's pretty cold out. Also, regardless of the fact that we have sewer issues, you may want to use the restroom now. Who knows when the next time we will have a semi-secure place to go will be."

"Yuck!" said Peggy with a grimace.

"Suck it up, Buttercup!" said Jason, trying his best to keep a straight face, but to no avail. They all busted out laughing together. They were thankful to have each other at that moment. It would be a totally different situation to have to face alone. Deep inside, each of them worried about their families back home, but they knew they had to focus on the moment to get there.

Chapter 4: Back on the Homefront

Just two days before, when the events began to unfold, Evan's wife, Molly, and their kids were at "The Homefront," which is how she and Evan lovingly referred to their little piece of rural Tennessee paradise. Molly, a homeschool parent, was logging into a co-op website for some daily participation in a natural science class for their son, Jake. She had just gotten the live feed up, when suddenly their internet service seemed to go down. She picked up her cell phone to call a neighbor who had the same service, which had been known to be troublesome in the past, only to find that her cellular service wasn't working either. There was no signal strength at all.

"Jake, just go ahead and take a second look over what you were supposed to discuss. That way, when it comes back on, you'll be prepared to jump right in. I'm going to check on the girls."

As Molly left the room and went down the hall, the lights suddenly went out and all of their appliances went silent. Fortunately, the power was only out for a brief moment; the diesel standby generator that Evan had insisted they invest in began to provide the home with uninterrupted power. She really started to wonder what was going on at that point.

"No internet, no cellular service, and now no power? What in the world could be going on?" she mumbled to herself.

Since her television had power with the generator being online, she checked their satellite TV service only to find that it was out too. This really concerned her, but she kept her worries to herself and decided to occupy the kids in the meantime by going outside and working with their animals. Their little hillbilly oasis gave them plenty of ways to stay busy.

In addition to meeting their sustenance and security needs, their kids also loved the property. Recreation opportunities abounded for the children. Jake, who was fourteen, found it a bit far from his friends, but since he had recently switched to homeschooling, the distance from their old home in Knoxville really wasn't that big of an issue. Evan and Molly's other two children, Lillian and Samantha, who were usually called Lilly and Sammy for short, were just two years and eight months of age respectively, so they really didn't know any different. Lilly was quite attached to her father. She clung to him while he was home and loved patrolling the property with her father on the family's ATV. She was truly growing up to be an outdoorsy little girl in the environment The Homefront provided.

They had a garden plot of about an acre, with lots of suitable land to expand into a more self-sustaining size if need be. This garden, in the meantime, would help them cultivate their farming skills while providing some fresh produce as a bonus. One of the first purchases they made after buying the property was a 1952 Ford 8N tractor. It was old and basic, but for their purposes, it was more than adequate. Its simplicity made it easy to keep running on a budget, or God forbid, in a post-collapse environment. Piece by piece, they also acquired a two-bottom turn plow, a disc cultivator, an aerator, a bush hog, a boom lift pole, a hay spear, and a finish mower for the tractor. All of this would be used to maintain the garden, as well as the rest of the property.

In addition to gardening for food, Molly had always wanted a milk cow since she had been raised on fresh cow's milk as a child, so a cow was added to the homestead. Luckily, the property had an existing barn and animal pens from the previous owners, making it a relatively simple addition for the Bairds.

Evan began raising rabbits for a renewable food source. He got the idea from his like-minded friend and coworker, Jason. Jason and his wife raised rabbits as an addition to their preps since their location did not allow for larger, traditional livestock. They loved the low-maintenance aspect of raising rabbits and found that, even though they lived in a suburban neighborhood, it was easily added as a backyard project. Jason's success with rabbits had motivated Evan to try it as an entry level livestock of sorts. Molly and Evan wanted to eventually raise cattle, pigs, and goats for meat, but they didn't want to take on too much until they were sure they could handle it all. With Evan's job as a pilot keeping him on the road a lot, Molly and the kids had to be able to handle it without him for up to a week at a time.

In addition to rabbits, they had a chicken coop up and running, providing themselves with fresh eggs and occasionally meat for the table. Like the rabbits, they saw this as an easy first step to having a working hobby farm. Molly also loved the idea of raising their three children in an environment where they could see where food really comes from and for them to be able to participate in the process as a learning experience. Evan and Molly both felt that American children were being raised in a world that was far too fragile, and knowing the basics of self-sufficiency could be key skills to have someday.

Their one hundred-acre property consisted of about thirty acres of cleared, rolling hills and seventy acres of a mix of partially wooded to densely wooded and hilly terrain. The house, barn, a large shop, and a tractor shed were all located on the cleared portion of the property. The remaining undeveloped land was not ideally suited for traditional farming, but it created an excellent natural buffer from the surrounding neighbors. It also provided a natural food source and habitat for deer, squirrel, wild rabbit, turkey, grouse, pheasant, and the occasional black bear. They considered this a God-given form of food storage.

The property was on its own water well and septic system, as well as having the benefit of a natural stream that flowed year-round. Although the stream wasn't large enough for fish, it made an ideal alternate water source, as well as contributing to the natural habitat that helped to bolster the wildlife population. They considered this when planning to make their home semi-off-grid. They hoped one day to make their home completely off-grid. However, that would be a project that would advance as time and money would allow.

Remotely located, the property had both benefits and drawbacks in regards to security. The benefit was that your average *"city rat"*—as Evan called the street thug, petty criminal types—that generally resided in urban areas—more than likely would not venture out that far, unless, of course, the situation declined to the point that a large scale migration took place. However, the more organized and tactically capable criminals may use the remoteness as cover for an assault on the property. This type of scenario could be a reality if a group wanted to take possession of the family's food and supplies in the event of a SHTF scenario where lawlessness ensued. For this potential eventuality, Evan had put a few things in place.

As an avid hunter and already being familiar with their use and concealment, Evan put hunting-style tree stands at various places around the property. This would not only allow them to utilize the natural cover of the woods for concealment, but they also provided elevated shooting and observation positions as well.

The elevated position of the tree stands, often on the ridge of the hill tops, also gave better range to the handheld radios that the family would be using around the property. This would enable a sentry to be able to communicate with the house, even when cell phone coverage was unavailable. Due to the nature of the terrain and the remoteness of their location, several locations on the property were cellular dead spots even when the commercial phone services were up and running. In these instances, the handheld radios would always be a basic necessity.

Evan numbered each stand and posted a corresponding map with the radio base station at the house so that a basic means of COMSEC (communication security) could be used without giving away the sentry's position in a situation where the frequency were to be compromised by a potential threat. A report such as *"we have a deer—or a herd of deer—near six"* would indicate that one or a group of people had been spotted by stand six. The phrase would include *"doe* or *does"* for unarmed and *"buck* or *bucks"* for armed individuals.

In the event the sentry needed to vacate the stand in a hurry, having been seen or needing to react to a potential situation, a climbing rig would be worn while in the stand. This would act as both a safety harness in the event of an accidental fall, as well as serving as an emergency egress device. The sentry could simply rappel down in a hurry on the side of the tree opposite the threat, using the tree for cover while leaving the area or reacting to the threat.

In addition to the observation stands, Evan used motion-activated hunting trail cameras in the more remote locations and wired security cameras closer to the house. The monitors for these cameras were co-located with the radio base station. Additionally, an infrared camera system was used on each side of the home for nighttime security. All of the cameras, the radio base station, and the handheld radio charging stations were primarily powered by a bank of batteries that were continuously trickle-charged on the house's emergency electrical circuit. This circuit was connected to normal house power with the automatic start and switchover diesel generator. This gave three levels of power continuity to the Baird's communication and observation security plan.

As for physical security, being a well-built, older brick home gave the structure a good, basic level of protection from both natural and criminal threats. The two aboveground floors were fortified with steel security doors that, to the average person, were merely normal decorative exterior doors. Evan also reinforced all of the door jams with steel hidden underneath decorative wood trim. Six welded steel hinges, painted to match the white trim, held the doors directly to the steel reinforcements. The idea was to keep the house from looking like a prison while providing an extra level of physical and ballistic strength. Any unsuspecting "city rat" that ventured out that far would have a rude awakening if they tried to kick in a door.

The exterior windows all looked normal to the naked eye. However, Evan had custom-made functional steel shutters covered with a decorative veneer. They could be closed when needed, essentially armor-plating the windows. Each side of each shutter also had a decorative cross designed into them to use as a shooting port once the glass window was opened from the inside. As a big fan of the western film genre, Evan admittedly borrowed this idea from the classic Clint Eastwood movie *The Outlaw Josey Wales.*

In addition to the hardened forms of physical security that the Bairds had installed, they also planted Pyracantha, or "firethorn bush," around all of the lower level windows. The firethorn bush contains thorns that leave a painful burning sensation on contact that lasts for hours. This would help create a natural defensive barrier that would merely look as if the Bairds had a penchant for landscaping rather than defense. Once a would-be intruder encountered the firethorn bushes, they would either retreat, regroup, or be somewhat contained for the Bairds to deal with as necessary.

In the event the Bairds needed to egress through one of their own lower level windows, they cut sheets of three-quarter inch thick plywood to the size of the windows and located several of them in convenient, yet out-of-the-way, locations around the home. They could then simply throw the plywood out the window, creating a bridge to clear the bushes on their way out. They knew the same tactic could also be employed by intruders attempting to enter the house in order to defeat the defensive nature of the firethorn bushes, but they figured this would at least keep the unprepared intruder at bay while they dealt with them. If a more planned and prepared team made a coordinated assault on the house, the bushes would more than likely only provide a minimal level of deterrence.

The finished basement was secure by design. The doors from the outside, as well as the inside of the house, were similarly reinforced, creating a safe room if someone breached the interior of the home. With that in mind, all of the communication and observation equipment was located there, as well as cots, food, water, medical supplies, and a gun safe. Additionally, the basement was separated into a main open space, a bathroom, and an additional room that could be used as a quiet room for sleeping or for additional storage. This was the planned "bug in" room during any security threat that didn't require or allow an evacuation of the home.

In regards to their defensive response capabilities, Evan had a substantial firearms and weapons collection that could be employed as necessary. His collection had been a work in progress for many years. He had numerous non-tactical firearms that included both classic and modern muzzle loaders, bolt-action hunting rifles in various calibers such as .30-06' Springfield, .308 Winchester, and .300 Winchester Magnum. In addition to these, he had a few lever-action cowboy style rifles chambered in calibers ranging from .45 Colt to .30-30 Winchester and a hard hitting, old school .45-70 Government. Evan fondly referred to his .45-70 as *"thumper"* due to its high mass projectiles traveling at low velocities. It was truly a knockdown rather than a shoot-through gun.

He had an assortment of tactical guns as well. A few years back, before the gun control scare of 2012, Evan had the foresight to pick up ten VZ2008 rifles, imported by Century Arms International (CAI), while they were going for just over three hundred dollars each. VZ2008s were CAI's sporting name for the Czechoslovakian made VZ58. The VZ58 was a rifle that the Czech's developed in order to play along with the Soviet's mandate of the use of the 7.62X39 intermediate cartridge. Unlike most available AKs and AKMs, VZs were made on a milled steel receiver rather than stamped sheet metal. They also had a very unique bolt design that opened the entire top of the receiver when cycling to eject the spent shell casing. This design had several benefits that attracted Evan. First, there was no exposed ejection port. The gun appeared to be completely sealed when the bolt was forward. This helped keep any loose debris, or other contamination, out of the weapon. Secondly, it seemed nearly impossible to get a fail-to-eject malfunction as the top of the gun was wide open during the rearward movement of the bolt, rather than merely having a constricted port to allow the spent casing to be expelled from the action. The VZ58 also had a last round bolt hold open, unlike the AK pattern rifles. This saves the step of cycling the action on reloads, as is required with the aforementioned design, as well as helping the user to immediately identify an empty magazine.

Basically, Evan felt that this design gave the quality and functional benefits of the AR platform, with the ballistics and the availability of the lower cost ammunition of the AK platform. After the gun control scare of 2012, 5.56/.223 had been very hard and expensive to come by, whereas 7.62X39 Russian was still widely available in bulk. Also, considering that steel-cased Russian ammo was nearly half the price of the quality brass-cased ammo that the AR platform needed for reliable function, it made the VZ58 economical to stock up for as well. Evan also stocked up on VZ58 magazines as they would not function in an AK/AKM platform rifle. He felt this would make any of their "throw down" mags useless to most adversaries as the VZ58 was nowhere near as proliferated as the AK/AKM.

Evan also had several AR and AK-based rifles. Most were in the common to the type calibers, but a few were in special configurations. He had one AR in .450 Bushmaster, one in .300 AAC Blackout, and one AR lower with a Tactilite T1 single-shot bolt-action .50 BMG upper. Each of these guns had their uses, but he planned on the VZs being his SHTF guns. He could outfit everyone at home with a matching gun, ammo, and magazines. Their small size and light weight, with the simple folding stock, made them ideal for all day carry, even by smaller framed family members and friends. The other rifles could, of course, be called upon when needed or when the conditions specified a particular round or capability.

When it came to handguns, Evan had myriad different revolvers and semi-automatics in his collection. However, he had been stocking up on 1911 platform handguns and magazines for SHTF ammo, parts, and magazine commonality. Having used M1911 pistols while serving as a member of the Naval Security

Force while on active duty just prior to the Navy's transition to the Beretta M-9 service pistol, Evan had always had a soft spot for them. Also, since he and Jake had used them as their main competition handguns for IDPA and IPSC matches, there seemed to be 1911 magazines, holsters, and accessories already in the home in such large quantities that it only seemed like the natural defensive choice.

While inside the home, Evan wanted his family, and anyone else who comes along and joins them in a potential SHTF scenario, to carry whatever they wanted, but outside of the home, he felt carrying a common type like the VZ58 and 1911 would alleviate any on-watch or fighting-in-position resupply issues.

Molly, who once felt like a majority of Evan's spending and preparations were a bit over the top, would soon come to appreciate the steps that he had gone through to give his family every possible advantage in uncertain times.

Chapter 5: The Journey Begins

The crew, which now included Damon Rutherford, gathered their things and put on their clothing in layers the best they could. Peggy jokingly said with a smile, "At least I don't have to worry about fashion today."

Jason responded, "Or anytime soon, for that matter." That cold, hard fact quickly extinguished her smile as it reminded her of their newfound reality. "Oh, sorry."

"No biggie," said Peggy. "I'll get used to it eventually. I just hope Zack and my parents are okay. I wonder if this is happening there."

"Well, once we get on the road I'm sure we will learn a few things along the way about what's going on in the rest of the country," Jason replied, hoping to make her feel better.

"Well, kids," Damon interrupted, "let's get going before our fan club comes back for our autographs. Jason, let's go with your plan. Peggy and I will stay out of the way while Evan is covering your climb down the fire escape, and then we'll follow on your signal."

"Roger that!" answered Jason, feeling excited to get going.

He quietly climbed down the fire escape with his pack on his back and his Sig holstered on his side while Evan covered him from above. He had to jump the last four feet to the ground as the fire escape did not reach all the way to the sidewalk below. Immediately upon reaching the ground, he drew his pistol and cleared the alley. Once he was reasonably sure the alley was clear, he gave Evan the thumbs-up for the rest to follow.

Evan whispered to Damon and Peggy, "Okay, there is a little jump at the bottom, but it's no big deal. You can toss your bags down to Jason at that point to ease the impact."

They both nodded and headed out the window. Peggy went down first and Damon followed her closely behind. They crept slowly down the fire escape, being careful not to make any unwanted sounds so as not to alert those in the building who had already proven to be a threat. They reached the last step and tossed their bags down to Jason one by one as he motioned for them.

Jason set their bags aside and signaled to them to jump on down. Since Peggy was in front of Damon on the narrow fire escape, she jumped first. Jason stood, ready to catch her fall if need be, but with her cushy running shoes, she made the landing just fine. Damon jumped next; upon landing, he winced in pain and fell to the ground.

"Are you okay?" asked Jason in a whisper.

"Yeah, just my damn bad knee. I'll survive," he answered as he struggled to his feet.

Jason then motioned for Evan to come on down. Evan holstered his pistol and slipped out the window. Just then, he heard a loud crack in the adjoining room they had vacated after the incident with the others. Almost immediately following that noise, he heard a blast from a shotgun, the cycling of a pump action, and then another shot. He hustled down the fire escape and quickly made the leap without hesitation. He landed in a roll and popped back up to his feet, pistol drawn and immediately covered the window above.

Meanwhile, Jason hurried Damon and Peggy behind a dumpster that was up against the hotel's exterior wall. *Anyone attempting to fire down from above at that angle will have to expose themselves to do so*, he thought to himself. Evan continued to cover the windows of the hotel while he moved to take position behind the dumpster with his crew. They heard a commotion above and then another big thump.

Evan turned to Jason and said, "Those idiots didn't know we had adjoining rooms and moved over one. Let's move while they are busy with that door. You take the lead, Jason. Damon and Peggy, you two follow him and watch for his signals. I'll cover you from the rear."

They all silently nodded, and the crew took off down the street, hugging the buildings for cover. Once they had gotten a few buildings away, they took shelter behind a convenience store that backed up to the Long Island Railway. The tracks were separated from the store by a tall chain-link fence that was entangled with what appeared to be many years of foliage growth.

Once Evan was sure they weren't being followed, he looked at Jason and said, "Okay, Jason, you're tactically in charge from here. Damon, you navigate for us since it's your route and plan. I'll keep up the rear."

Jason said, "Roger Roger," as he often does in a sharp manner. "Okay then," he said to the group, "we've got good cover here. Let's lie low for a bit to make sure we aren't being followed. Damon, use this time to get your bearings and get us a route."

Damon fumbled around in his bag for a second, then produced a map. Evan said, "Wow! A paper map."

Damon responded, "Yep, I'm old school. I don't wanna get into that smartphone mess, so I get a street map for everywhere I go."

"Thank God," Evan said. "My stupid smart phone with turn-by-turn directions isn't gonna do me any good now. Even if I had a signal, my battery died yesterday."

Damon grinned then went back to his map. After a few moments of studying the map and using the railroad as a way to gain his bearings, Damon said, "Okay, I've got it! Two blocks that way and we will come up on the POW/MIA Memorial Highway. The sun will start coming up in a few minutes, so just in case those hotel bastards are looking for us, let's try to at least make it that far while we have the darkness for cover. By the time we get to the POW/MIA, we will be far enough away for it not to matter."

"That's the plan then," said Jason. "Let's move. We will leapfrog every time we have to cross a street or an alley where we will be exposed. I'll make the first bound across while Evan covers me. We will then both cover the two of you. Then I will cover Evan. Let's just keep that movement pattern going unless I say otherwise. Watch for my signals and try to stay as quiet as possible." He then gave Damon and Peggy a quick, down-and-dirty review of the basic hand signals he would be using. He limited it to the basics like look, halt, down, advance, retreat, rally, listen, etc.

Once everyone was clear on what was expected of them, Jason led the way by crossing the street first. Upon reaching the other side of the street, he gave the signal to advance. Damon and Peggy made the crossing and then he signaled to Evan to advance as well. "Okay, that was good. Let's keep that going," he told them once Evan had joined up with them.

Evan chimed in and said, "Damon, you look like you were limping when you guys crossed the street. Are you still hurting from the fall?"

"Yes, but I'll survive. I mean, I have to, so to hell with the pain. I'll let you know if it becomes too much to bear, otherwise don't slow down for me."

"Roger Roger," said Jason and off he went.

They all followed between two buildings to get to the next street over. As Jason sliced the pie around the building with his Sig drawn and at the low ready, he saw the smoldering ruins of a car parked sideways in the middle of the street. He motioned for the rest of the group to advance and rally on him, and they complied, being as stealthy as possible. Once they caught up with him and they were all crouched together in a huddle, he quietly said, "Look at this crap. This must be one of the explosions we heard. It almost looks like it was parked there and blown up on purpose to block the street."

"That would explain the lack of vehicle traffic we've seen if whoever is responsible for this has done it in other places strategically as well," replied Evan. "Not to mention the psychological effect it would have on the general population at large. Make people afraid of IEDs like they've seen on the evening news of places in Iraq and Afghanistan for the past decade, and people will think twice about being out and about. We always talk about taking the fight to the enemy, and it looks like the enemy has followed that doctrine and brought it right back to us."

"Okay, enough sight-seeing, let's move," commanded Jason. He then made a bound over to the next street, and like a smooth, well-trained unit, they all followed upon his signal.

Once they regrouped, Damon said, "Okay, the next road over is the POW/MIA. If this street looks safe enough to you, lets handrail it from here for a while. Staying on a residential street would give us better cover opportunities than a main thoroughfare."

"Makes sense to me," replied Jason.

"Me too," said Evan.

"Okay," said Jason, ready and anxious to get moving. "Now that the sun is coming up, let's just walk down the sidewalk as if we are supposed to be here. Evan and I will take our normal positions as point and rear with our guns holstered and hidden. You two stick together in the middle, but keep your distance from us in the event Evan or I have issues to deal with. If something happens, take cover and follow our signals, or do what you need to do if we are no longer in the fight. At least if we are spread out we all won't encounter the same threat at once."

"You mean like IEDs?" questioned Peggy.

"Yeah, or people, or aliens, or zombies, or whatever else is causing this crap. Personally, I'm hoping for zombies, but it's more than likely aliens," Jason said with a straight face.

"Ha ha," she said sarcastically.

They all shared a laugh, then Jason said, "Okay, let's get going."

The next few miles were relatively uneventful. Jason kept his appropriate distance ahead of Damon and Peggy, and Evan kept his distance to the rear with both men being able to cover the entire group's movement. The sun was now fully up and the neighborhoods were starting to stir. There were steel trash cans and car tire rims on the sidewalk with fires set inside. Some people were huddled around them for warmth.

Jason made the rally signal and the group formed up. He said, "Now that the sun is up and people are out and about, it would probably be okay to go ahead and walk together for a while. We are sort of figuring out the whole situation as we go. Evan and I will still take the front and the rear, but we can keep a closer gap so that we can communicate. There probably isn't as much chance of being bothered in the broad daylight."

As they continued down the street, what appeared to be a MRAP (Mine Resistant Armor Protected Vehicle) with Department of Homeland Security (DHS) markings, drove by a crossing street in the distance. It then made a turn onto the street just paralleling them. Damon said, "Oh, here we go."

As the vehicle approached the crew, it began playing a recorded message over the loudspeaker. The message said, "Attention, the United States is under a state of emergency. By order of the president, all food, water, and medical supplies are to be surrendered to the nearest FEMA Emergency Response Unit. FEMA Emergency Response Units are being set up in each burrow and county. More information will be provided upon surrender of said items. Failure to comply will be dealt with under the strictest penalty of the law in accordance with the executive orders of the president. All persons are hereby ordered to remain indoors unless transiting to a FEMA location as directed."

As the truck went by, Jason said, "What the hell? Who do they think they are saying that you have to turn in all of your food and water? How the heck are you supposed to survive?"

"You survive at their discretion," Damon chimed in. "He who controls the food, controls the people. Just remember how the Soviets did in Russia. They starved out the towns where there was resistance to their brutal regime while rewarding those who supported them. It's a pretty basic dictatorial tactic. Besides, Executive Order 10988 gives the president the ability to seize all food, food production, food distribution assets, and so on. And that's not all, Executive Order 10997 gives him the power to seize all fuels and forms of energy, and Executive Order 10999 gives him the power to seize all transportation assets. Looks like he finally found an excuse to use them. They may only be talking about food now, but they will get to the other ones soon if I had my guess."

"Well, we've gotta keep up the pace then," said Evan in a very agitated manner. "This urban hell and others like it will be easier for them to control right off the bat. They won't worry about the rural areas until they've got these places locked down."

Peggy responded in a stressed voice, "But I don't get it. Where are the regular police? Why aren't they the ones handling all of this?"

"My guess is they are at home with their families protecting them. That and the federal government doesn't have direct control over local police, unless, of course, the politician that appointed the chief of police is in bed with them politically. But as far as sheriffs go, they are constitutionally elected office holders and answer only to the people. So if the government wants to get heavy-handed, using their own forces is the surefire method to get the compliance that they may not automatically get from the locals," answered Damon.

About another mile down the street, the neighborhood started to deteriorate into an economically depressed area. Evan and Jason began to notice that most homes had bars on the windows and there was graffiti all over all of the dumpsters and most of the store fronts. They began to get an uneasy feeling by the change in their surroundings.

Evan said, "Okay, we need to jog over a street or two to get out of this rat hole before something happens."

Peggy looked at Evan. "Rathole? Are you some kind of racist or something?"

"No, not at all, Peggy. It's got nothing to do with race, and everything to do with reality," Evan replied. "I don't care what color the people are who live here. To put it plain and simple, if we were walking through a neighborhood of multi-million dollar homes, we wouldn't be in any danger. Those people, whether scum bags or not, probably have the means to continue to provide for themselves for a while. I would say their personal chef has the pantry stocked quite well. However, in this neighborhood, these people were probably barely getting by when things were good. No doubt, some are good people who, for whatever reason, never got out of this sort of situation in life. Others are just dirtbags who are in this place for a reason. They probably already didn't have anything extra. So when everything started to fall apart a few days ago, they were most likely down to their last loaf of bread. By about now, they are probably getting desperate. Short of some magical FEMA office showing up to feed them with food they confiscate from us, these people are probably at a breaking point. We don't want to be the ones they try and hit up for food because I doubt it will be a friendly request. It's gonna be dog-eat-dog around here soon, and I'd say some of the dogs around here are already rabid."

Peggy seemed to understand what Evan said, although the expression on her face made it evident that she didn't want to accept the reality of such things.

They took a crossing street to try to get a block over while still heading west in order to handrail the POW/MIA. As they walked around a corner, a group of men ranging from their late teens to their late twenties stepped out of the alley and said, "Hey, who the hell do you think you are coming through our hood without paying the toll?"

"Toll?" Jason said. "We didn't see any signs for a toll."

"Well here is your sign." The thug who seemed to be the alpha male pulled a three-foot long piece of pipe out from behind his back. The other men then began to block them in by taking up a position around them in an intimidating manner.

Evan said, "I don't think you really want to go there. I promise you, we won't pay a toll."

"Take their shit and cut that—"

POP! POP! POP!

Before the man could finish his sentence, Evan drew his pistol and put three rounds directly into his chest. One of the other men pulled out a pistol grip pump shotgun from a gym bag, but before he got it in a position to fire, Jason put two rounds into his chest, throwing him back onto the ground. Another of the men went for the shotgun and Evan and Jason both tore into him with their .40s, putting at least four shots into his torso. He fell dead on top of the other assailant with both men bleeding out so profusely, the pool of blood beneath them ran out onto the pavement like a scene from a Tarantino movie. Realizing they had messed with the wrong people, the other thugs turned and ran as fast as they could.

Evan and Jason were both high on an adrenaline rush like they had never felt. They wanted to finish off the whole group, but since the men turned coward and ran, they knew it was not the right thing to do. The attack was stopped, and that was what really mattered. In this state of things, though, they knew leaving guys like this out there to terrorize the next group of passersby didn't feel right, but they had a mission and they needed to get on the move before their gunshots attracted any unwanted attention from other armed thugs or authorities. This was not a good time to get into a tangle with law enforcement or locals. Do what you need to do, then press on was the prudent course of action.

Jason grabbed Peggy by the arm as she stood, frozen in shock from what had just happened. "C'mon, we gotta go." They all took off running down the street for a few blocks and then cut another street over before they slowed down.

Evan noticed that Damon's limp seemed to be getting worse after the run. He said, "Are you okay, man?"

"Yeah, yeah," he replied. "I'll keep it together. Besides, once we get to the boat, I can just kick back on the bridge and drive. I only have to hold out until then."

Jason turned to Evan and said, "Hammer pairs, man, hammer pairs. You're wasting ammo!"

"Yeah I know, I just get caught up in things and wanna shoot till he drops. I'll get it together for next time."

"Next time? Next time?" Peggy shouted. "What's wrong with you two? Why does everything have to end up in a gunfight?"

Jason responded sharply, "Peggy, we could just let you negotiate for us the next time some dirtbags want to rob us and do who knows what else. Do you remember the last time you saw a regular cop around here, or anyone else in uniform?" He didn't need to wait for her answer. "Me neither, and the other people around here are noticing it too. I don't know how many times we have to go through this with you, but in a situation like this, if you aren't aggressive enough, you won't make it very far."

Damon interjected, "Yep, it's like Marine Corps General James Mattis said, 'Be polite and professional, but have a plan to kill everyone you meet.'"

With that, Jason turned to Damon and said, "Here, I got you a present." He handed Damon the pistol-grip pump shotgun he grabbed from the dead assailant as they ran from the scene.

"Thanks!" Damon said. He looked it over and said, "A Mossberg 500. Nice! Looks like a full tube of ammo is in it too. It's the extended tube, so eight in the pipe and one in the chamber for nine rounds."

"Sorry, I didn't have time to search the guy for more ammo," Jason said. "But even with just one loaded magazine tube of ammo, it's better than nothing. The way things are getting, you're likely to use it sooner rather than later."

Chapter 6: The Jones Home

The morning of Jason's flight, a few days earlier, had started out as a normal day back at the Jones household. Jason left a little early to swing by Evan's hotel to pick him up for their trip while Jason's wife, Sarah, got their two boys ready for school. Wrangling two rambunctious young boys in the morning while trying to get ready for work could be quite a chore, and that day they had put her a few steps behind. She dropped them off at school on her way to work at the Belleau Woods Apartments, where she was the front office manager. Since she didn't get off until five o'clock in the afternoon on the average day, the boys would simply ride the school bus to the apartment complex along with the other kids who lived there.

Today was her least favorite day of the month at work. It was the day she had to knock on doors and post late notices for those residents who were two weeks or more behind. With the economy the way it was, her delinquent list seemed like it got longer each month. She dreaded the possible confrontations and excuse-filled stories she would get. She had heard it all over the two years since she started working there. With the unemployment rate being so high in Ohio and only getting worse, she truly had sympathy for them. How would she handle it if she and Jason were faced with the same situation? How would they be able to face their children when it came time for a potential eviction? Seeing the heartbreak and embarrassment in the eyes of people who had to face this dilemma was often too much to bear.

She saved her "bad news" rounds to do last that day. She didn't want to be in the middle of a heated discussion when her sons got off the bus, so she figured if she posted them on the doors on her way out, she wouldn't have to deal with anyone until the next day. She met them at the bus stop and led them to the playground, where they could play until she made her rounds. She welcomed them with their usual group hugs and kisses and said, "Oh, my handsome little boys, how I've missed you. Mommy loves you so much."

They both smiled and said, "Love you too, Mommy!"

As they walked to the playground, she asked, "So how was your day?"

Michael, their older son, responded, "It was good until we got on the bus."

"What do you mean until you got on the bus?" she said.

"Well, one of the older kids called you some bad names and said you've been bothering his mom, making her mad. He said when she gets mad she takes it out on him. He said you better stop, or he will kick my butt until you do. Only he used a different word for butt that I can't say."

"Oh, Michael," she said, "I'm so sorry he said that to you, but it's Mommy's job to make sure people know they have to pay their rent. If people don't pay their rent, the apartments would have to close and then where would everybody stay?"

He shrugged his shoulders as if he understood. She said, "Why don't you boys just play in the office break room, and I'll be back in just a few minutes." Considering the event on the school bus, she figured they would be better off not going to the playground until she finished her rounds.

Once she began her rounds, she made it all the way through the first building uneventfully. There were just a few two-week late notices there. The eviction notice she had to post was in the next building over. As she started up the stairs of the second building, the lights flickered, then went out. The battery-powered emergency lights kicked on, but since they were not good for long, she felt as if she had been saved by the bell. *I'll just tell the manager that I couldn't finish because of the power outage, and since I'm off tomorrow, maybe he will do it for me*, she thought. With a little more spring in her step, she headed back to the office to gather her boys and head for home.

As she neared the office, she ran into a tenant by the name of

Mark Platt. Mark was one of those fellows who would rope you into a conversation and never let you go. Attempting to avoid eye contact, she tried to walk on by when he said, "Mrs. Jones, did you hear about the plane crash?"

This immediately caught her attention. "What?"

"Well, I was watching the news where a passenger plane had crashed somewhere around New York. I couldn't catch the whole story, though, because that's when the power went out. My phone is dead, too, so I thought since your husband is a pilot, you may know what's going on."

Fear and anxiety swept through her body as she realized Jason was flying to New York that day and that she hadn't heard from him. She checked her phone, but she had no missed calls. She noticed she didn't have a signal either. She turned back to Mark. "When you said that your phone was dead, did you mean your battery or your signal?"

"My signal. Why?"

Oh my God, she thought. *Could all of Jason and Evan's paranoia be right? Was something happening? Was he okay?*

Sarah left Mark standing there as she picked up her pace and jogged back to the office. When she arrived, she found her boys sitting out front due to the electricity being out. She grabbed them both and rushed to the car. She drove straight for home but remembered she had neglected to stop for gas that morning, as she was running late. A few miles from their neighborhood, she pulled into a gas station and noticed a sign that said, "We apologize for the inconvenience, but due to the power outage we are unable to dispense fuel." She immediately got back on the road and continued toward home, constantly checking the fuel gauge.

After another two miles, the car started to shudder and the sound of the engine was soon replaced by the tone of the systems monitor annunciators; she had run out of gas. Sarah coasted to the side of the road, got out, and looked in the cargo pod that Jason had installed on the top of their car. There she found a five-gallon can of gas, as well as a few other "just in case" items. *Plenty to make it home*, she thought as she poured the contents of the gas can into the fuel tank. "Oh, Jason," she mumbled to herself, "I love your annoying paranoia."

They arrived home to find the power out there, as well. She fired up the portable gasoline generator in the garage and ran an extension cord to the television. To her dismay, she saw that every channel was nothing but static. *Well*, she thought, *at least if it's happening, the boys and I are in a good place thanks to Jason and his crazy prepping*. She was far better equipped to handle what was going on than the average family. Although their home wasn't upgraded with the security enhancements that the Baird household had, they had plenty of food, water, weapons, and about every other survival supply she and the boys would need.

A little over four hundred miles separated the Baird and Jones families. Since the Baird's Homefront had everything they would need—and more—to hold out for a longer duration of time, Evan and Jason had mutually planned on having the Jones family bug out to Tennessee to join the Bairds should the need arise. Not only did they share operational security (OPSEC) type information and planning, they kept each other focused on their preps by sharing and recommending related reading materials and ideas; they were basically long-distance prepping partners.

Like Evan, Jason had quite the gun collection. Although they both had numerous non-matching guns and calibers at their disposal, they would joke "disturbed minds think alike" as they both chose the 7.62X39 Russian and .45ACP as their primary defensive cartridges. Jason didn't catch the VZ58 bug like Evan had, but over the past year, he had been scouring gun shows and the like to find off-the-record SKSs to stock up on. While the cost for an SKS was a lot higher than in previous years, they were still less expensive than AR and some AK platform rifles.

Jason also liked the conventional, old school rifle layout of the SKS. Also, with the ability to fit them with thirty-round magazines and optics, he felt they were his best of both worlds. In addition, since the SKS utilizes the same 7.62X39 cartridge as Evan's VZs, he and Evan were stockpiling the same ammunition. If things ever came to pass where the two families needed to hook up, the collections would complement each other.

Jason's handgun collection, like Evan's, also revolved around the venerable 1911. This gave them commonality in that regard, as well. Jason's specialty rifle was his modified and customized Remington Model 700 in .300 Winchester Magnum. His "Remy" had been a pet project of sorts. He had used an M24 based on the Remington 700 while he was in the Army, filling the role of company designated sharpshooter, and felt right at home with the design. He had never officially gone to sniper training due to Clinton-era budget cuts. In addition, he was not the kind of soldier who would cultivate the right relationships for the benefit of his career, and in his opinion, most of the Sniper, Ranger, and SPECOPS school slots were reserved for guys who were buddies with all of the right brass. That was the dilemma of serving during sustained peacetime; those who made the calls weren't necessarily making decisions based on really getting the job done.

Jason had taken on gunsmithing as a hobby and as an unofficial preparedness skill. He had been working on his rifle on and off over the past few years. It had a stock that fully floated the barrel from Accuracy International, a custom long-range barrel, threaded for use with a suppressor that he had quietly "acquired", and a match-grade custom trigger job that broke as smoothly as glass. A Night Force 5-25X56 scope rounded out the package. Combined, these modifications made an easy-to-carry, reliable "reach out and touch someone" gun.

Jason understood his role in the SHTF plan he and Evan constructed; as the one who would be on the move for the meet up, instead of stockpiling weapons based on sheer numbers like Evan had, Jason focused on having what he needed to be well armed on the road. Six SKSs for close-in fighting, six 1911 handguns, and his Remington would round out his firearms in the event of a bug out. He just couldn't carry very many different types of ammunition and magazines, as well as the other food and supplies he would need for the journey, without overloading his bug out vehicle.

The Jones' family bug out vehicle was Jason's 1999 Dodge Ram 2500 long bed crew cab 4X4. Powered by a 5.9L Cummins Turbo Diesel engine, his truck had plenty of power. The Cummins was famous for its bulletproof reliability and relatively good fuel economy for a truck of that size. Diesel engines, being very fuel-flexible, also made this truck the ideal choice for a future with a potentially unreliable fuel supply and availability. Being the heavier built 2500 chassis with a sturdy Dana 60 front axle and a Dana 70 in the rear, his truck gave him a drivetrain that could take emergency abuse, as well as the ability to carry a heavy load with little stress on the components. Additionally, Evan's personal truck was a 2001 Cummins-powered Dodge 4X4, giving them parts-commonality once the families linked up. Though not as roomy as a more modern crew cab, the extended cab configuration provided them with adequate passenger room for Jason, Sarah, and their two sons.

When Jason bought the truck, the previous owner had already installed a fiberglass truck bed canopy. This would make the bed of the truck a useful sleeping and equipment storage space. One of Jason's first modifications was that he installed a cargo rack, which was elevated above the canopy by a steel tube on each corner of the bed. The rack would make the perfect spot for full-size spare tires and other bulky items.

He didn't like the thought of his family sleeping in potentially hostile environments with nothing but fiberglass or thin sheet metal to protect them, so he devised a way to have on-demand armor for the bed area. He cut four pieces of three-eighth inch steel plate. Two of the pieces were cut to the dimensions of the front and back of the canopy. The other two were cut to the dimensions of the sides. In the sheets of steel, he drilled holes that corresponded with the holes he had drilled into the steel tubes supporting the rack. He then installed studs into the holes on the tubes and attached wing nuts to them so there would be no need for hardware or tools, which may not be available at a critical time.

Each piece of steel was then welded to hinges that were attached to the longitudinal and lateral main tubes of the rack. Each of these "poor man's instant up-armor" sheets of steel, as he put it, would be folded up when not in use. Since the sheets lay on top of the rack, they were nearly out of sight, except, of course, for the front piece between the canopy and the cab of the truck; it was simply bolted permanently in place. Before installing it permanently, Jason cut a hole in it that corresponded with the sliding rear window on his truck and the sliding window on the canopy. This was to ensure access to the cab of the truck from the bed. Then, when the need arose, he could move what was on top of the rack, flip the sides back down, and secure the wing nuts, creating a temporary ballistic shelter for the occupants of the truck bed. The rack itself would act as a shelter for the top of the canopy to protect against falling debris.

In the bed of the truck, he built an elevated platform made from a lightweight aluminum frame covered with half-inch plywood. This platform sat level with the bed rails and made a cramped, but functional, sleeping space during their potential journey south to meet up with the Baird family. This would also keep the sleeping family members elevated to the level of the retractable steel doors, providing much more protection than the truck bed itself. Below this platform was the storage space for the necessary food, clothing, medical supplies, hygiene supplies, ammunition, and anything else they may need to bring along, depending on the time of year.

He kept the truck looking mostly stock to avoid drawing too much attention either from overzealous, post-event government personnel, or from those who may simply want to take what they have. He did, however, equip it with receiver hitch bumpers front and rear for use with a Warn 12,000 lb. winch that he had mounted on a receiver-ready platform. This way, the winch could remain hidden in the cargo compartment of the truck until needed and could be used on either the front or rear of the truck, depending on the situation at hand.

Other tactical modifications that wouldn't draw too much attention included run-flat, all-terrain tires with a full-sized spare, mounted on a Jeep style swing-away tire carrier, which was attached to the rear bumper. There was also an auxiliary fifty-gallon fuel tank hidden underneath the truck, between the frame and the body. Jason didn't want to be too obvious that he had extra fuel, such as if he had to carry it in gas cans on the outside of the vehicle in plain view. He knew that fuel would be a critical, highly sought after item in any post-event scenario.

With thirty-five gallons of fuel in the factory tank, plus fifty gallons in his auxiliary tank—at a very conservative estimated fuel economy of thirteen miles per gallon while the truck is loaded down—the Jones family should be able to make the complete distance to East Tennessee without stopping for fuel. Jason installed an older style, manual fuel feed changeover valve underneath the driver's seat, allowing him to switch from one tank to the other without having to stop.

The Jones family had about two years' worth of food stores and myriad medical and hygiene supplies located at their Zanesville home, just in case the option of traveling to the planned bug out location down south in Tennessee became untenable. After all, being a former infantryman, Jason well understood that no battle plan ever survives the first contact with the enemy. His mantra was, "Have a plan, then have a backup plan, then be prepared to act without a plan. Have whatever you need, to do whatever you must, whenever you must."

Chapter 7: The Journey Continues

The morning's events left the crew with a mixed bag of emotions. Their victories in dealing with scumbags looking for easy prey was confidence boosting and yielded an extra weapon for Damon to carry; however, taking a human life, no matter how worthless it seemed at the moment, still haunted the men deep inside. They were motivated and dedicated to the cause of getting home to their families, helping them to be able to compartmentalize the negative emotions from the events. They used their crude sense of humor and their victories to bolster the morale of their team.

The men also knew they had to keep moving and keep up their positivity for the sake of Peggy. Peggy was simply not prepared for the events that had unfolded during this supposedly routine New York City layover. Her entire world had changed in an instant, and she had never considered the possibility of anything like this happening. She had lived her life as the typical American, focusing only on the pop culture headlines that pervaded the American media, while ignoring politics and world events. Add to that, the emotional turmoil that resulted from her very recent and painful divorce, leaving her as a single mother, and she just didn't have a lot left in her to deal with all of it.

They kept up the pace, only occasionally stopping to check their position on Damon's map. Since they were hand railing their intended route, they needed to cross reference the street they were on with the map to make sure they weren't drifting away from their intended direction of travel. Being on foot, they needed to keep their diversions to a minimum, especially considering Damon's knee injury.

As the next hour passed, they saw desperate people trying to make sense of everything. Some were just staring out their apartment windows; others were in the street begging neighbors and passersby for any sort of food or water. Evan thought to himself how sad it was that people had gotten accustomed to not having more than one or two days' supply of food and water in their home. Some people probably had no water stored at all, as they depended on the supply of city water to their apartment for all of their needs. A refrigerator full of sodas wouldn't keep people hydrated very well now that their water supply was out. Modern society's reliance on "the system" taking care of them had turned people into nothing more than ants who couldn't survive without their colony.

It was approaching noon and the crew needed to stop for a quick break. Jason looked at Damon and said, "So, where we at, Boss?"

Damon said, "We are on Doxsey Place and should be coming up on Atlantic Ave. There is a baseball field and recreation area up ahead by an elementary school. Let's see if there is a place we can take a seat in that park area far enough away from people that they don't see us eating. The last thing we need right now is someone wanting our food. That park is the only spot I see with a little room to get off of the street."

"Sounds like a plan," Evan replied.

As they came upon the intersection of Doxsey and Atlantic, Evan said, "Okay, let's hold up here for a bit. Let's not just walk straight into the park. Let's observe and make sure we aren't going to be walking right into another toll booth to use the park."

"Good idea," Jason replied. "I'll hang a left on Atlantic and circle around the park to the other side. Once you see me on the opposite side of the field, I'll signal if it's clear and you can bring the others."

Evan nodded in agreement, and Jason went on his way. As Jason worked his way around the park, just off of Raymond Avenue, he saw something behind and up against the baseball field's home plate fence. His heart skipped a beat and his knees got weak as a dark feeling come over him, fearing that he knew exactly what it was. He climbed the short chain link fence separating the park from the street and slowly approached. The crew could see him climb the fence, but he was too far away to really see what he was up to.

Peggy said, "What's he doing?"

"Oh, he is just checking the place out really good for us. He will only be a minute," replied Evan who, deep down inside, also wondered what Jason may be up to.

As Jason approached the backstop fence, his fears became reality. A young Hispanic girl, probably no more than fifteen or sixteen years of age, lay there silent and still, wearing nothing but a shirt. The rest of her clothes seemed to have been torn from her and just tossed aside. He was certain she was dead. It looked as though she had been severely beaten and, he could only assume, raped. He reached down to check her pulse on her wrist and she was cold. Emotions swirled around in his mind from rage to sadness. He wanted to break down and cry and snap and kill every scumbag in this area. *This must have happened last night,* he thought. Thoughts of vigilante justice raged in his head. He wanted to hide nearby until dark and see what kind of rats came out of the woodwork and just kill them all. *Guilt by association,* he thought. *If they knew this body was here, then they knew what happened and were guilty.*

His rage was tempered as his thoughts turned to his wife and sons and what they may be going through at that very moment. His rage and sadness turned into determination. Determination to get to his family, return Peggy to hers, and then get the hell down to Tennessee where they could hold out and forget this nasty world exists. He jumped to his feet and got in the open so that Evan could see him. He signaled to avoid the park and to head down Atlantic one more block.

"Come on," Evan said. "The park is no good. He wants us to go around."

"What? Why?" Peggy questioned.

"Just trust him, Peggy," insisted Evan.

They proceeded with caution down Atlantic Avenue where Jason met them in front of an apartment complex. Jason looked clearly shaken and enraged. "What was it?" asked Damon.

"No stopping for Sunday picnics," said Jason in a short, harsh tone. "We aren't stopping until the boat."

Peggy started to ask Jason something, and Evan signaled her to hush and to just get going. He knew Jason, and for him to be that disturbed he knew it was something they didn't need to see. He was sure Jason would tell him eventually. No reason to bring it up now and just give Peggy something else to worry about.

"Damon, do you want to work up a new route from here?" asked Evan as they followed Jason's quickened pace.

"Sure thing," he replied. "It looks like if we keep going straight, we will come up on Union Avenue; if we hang a left there, it will take us down to Rockaway Road. A right turn on Rockaway Road will get us back to where we want to be."

"Roger Roger," said Jason, and the group continued on behind him with Evan, once again, taking up his position in the rear.

They were now in an area that was mostly comprised of middle class, single-family homes. They had been making good time, and Damon seemed to be hanging in there despite his bad knee. They saw a DHS MRAP enter the road from a side street. Jason immediately signaled for the group to cover to the right. He led them quickly down a side road and onto a smaller street that traveled away from Union Avenue.

Peggy asked, "Why are we hiding from the police?"

"Those are the same thugs who want us to turn our food and water in for government redistribution. They are also the same thugs who are being used impose martial law on the people here. We don't have a good explanation as to why we are traveling through here, and we definitely don't have a good explanation as to why we are carrying guns; even when not under some sort of martial law, they are strictly forbidden here," Evan explained. "Don't get me wrong, there are some damn fine men and women in law enforcement. We don't have to worry about them, but remember, every government that has committed tyrannical acts against its own people throughout history has had no shortage of people in uniform willing to do their dirty deeds. A politician can't force his will on the people without an armed man on the street to make it happen. Trust has to be earned in these situations on a case by case basis."

"Oh yeah," she said. "Sorry."

"Damon, where does this lead?" he then asked.

Damon shuffled his map around and said, "Just keep going straight, and this will get us back on Broadway, which was Plan A."

"Good deal," Evan replied.

As they continued, they could hear the loudspeaker from the DHS truck making the same demands for the confiscation of food, water, and medical supplies. Only now, the recording added the warning that all roads are closed to any non-government vehicles due to the state of emergency, and that all civilian use of motorized transportation is prohibited in the New York City area.

"Well, between that and the IED-ravaged cars, that explains the lack of vehicle traffic we've seen," Jason said.

Damon said, "Yeah, that and there probably aren't many operative gas stations with the power being down."

"I would bet that, and the Feds have probably seized the ones that are operating on generators," replied Evan.

"You guys probably have aluminum foil inside your pilot hats when at work, don't you?" Peggy joked. She then added, "You know, to keep the government from reading your minds or something crazy like that. You're just three peas in a pod."

They all shared a laugh and continued until they reached Broadway. From there, they resumed their original course. After a few more minutes, they came upon a convenience store with a crowd in front. The crowd seemed agitated and stressed. They could tell something serious was going on. Jason signaled the crew to cover to the right in order to observe out of sight for a moment before proceeding.

There was what appeared to be a DHS SUV parked to the side of the building and two DHS officers standing at the front of the store. The officers wore riot gear and looked like they meant business. They were arguing with the people who were clearly there for the food inside the store. The windows of the store had already been broken in. After a minute of arguing, they saw a DHS officer carry the remaining food from the store and load it into the back of the SUV. That made three officers that they could see at this point. The crowd looked as though they were demanding the food. As one young man reached and tried to take a loaf of bread, one of the other DHS officers fired on him at point-blank range with his AR-15 patrol rifle, shooting him directly in the chest.

"Holy Shit!" said Jason.

The crew was stunned. Just as the people began to scatter, the officer fired another four rounds into the fleeing crowd, dropping a young woman and an elderly man to the pavement where they lay limp and lifeless.

Outraged and disgusted, Jason looked at Evan and Damon and said, "Do you two want to live reckless and dangerous for a moment?"

"If it involves what I think you are saying, hell yes!" answered Evan. "Those bastards flat out murdered those people for that food, and if we don't do something about it, those won't be the last citizens they terrorize."

"Not to mention the fact that their vehicle can accelerate this journey for us," added Damon. "With all of the helicopters buzzing around, one of those DHS trucks will be the only way to drive the streets unnoticed, and this place is going to hell in a hurry. Let's right this wrong and take that thing and get the hell to the dock ASAP!"

"Okay, then, let's do it," Jason said. "Damon, collect everyone's food and put it in one pack. As they drive this way, walk out into the street with the backpack held over your head. When they stop, tell them you are just turning in your food as ordered. Act sheepish and scared so that their dominant attitude causes them to drop their guard. Give Evan your shotgun and put his .40 in the back of your waistband, just in case we don't get the job done. They've got body armor on and have ARs; we can't just take them on in a straight up gunfight, so here is the plan."

He whispered his idea to the men then asked Peggy to sneak around behind the adjacent house and told her not to come out until they called for her. "If you don't hear one of our voices calling you by name after the shooting stops, then just go and get away from here. Head toward the boat like we discussed and, if at all possible, we will meet up with you there," he said.

"Okay," she mumbled in a state of fear and disbelief. She slipped around behind the house and hid in the backyard as instructed.

As the SUV headed toward them down the road, Evan crawled up underneath a Toyota Four Runner SUV that was parked along the curb while Jason quietly opened the door and slipped into the back seat area. Damon walked out into the street carrying the backpack full of their food and lifted it above his head. He limped a little more than usual, putting on an act of weakness to get the murderous officers to lower their guard and underestimate him.

The DHS SUV pulled up in front of Damon in the middle of the street and turned its blue flashing lights on. Over the PA, they said, "Halt; state your intentions."

Damon replied, "I'm just turning in my family's food as ordered, sir."

"Lay the backpack on the street, empty its contents, and then take three paces backward. Keep your hands on top of your head and stay there until you're told otherwise."

Damon complied, and the officers exited the truck. The officers walked to within five feet of the Toyota SUV. One of them went to inspect the pack, another covered Damon, and the third officer appeared to be keeping his eye on the windows of neighborhood homes. *Perhaps feeling the guilt of what they had done was making him paranoid*, Evan thought. He could see them clearly while hiding behind the tire of the SUV from underneath.

As the officer sent to inspect the pack leaned down and looked at the contents scattered on the ground, he turned around and said, "Yep, it's food. Mostly tuna and stuff."

At that instant, a loud *BOOM* came from the underside of the Toyota as Evan fired the shotgun directly at the ankles of the officer covering Damon. The blast tore his left foot clean off and shredded the other. The sweeping action of the blast knocked the man's legs out from under him, sending him straight to the ground. Evan immediately racked another round into the chamber and took the feet out from under the second officer as well. Jason kicked the rear driver's side door open and fired at the officers while they were on the ground. As the officer in front of Damon spun around to engage Evan and Jason, Damon pulled the pistol out from his waistband and shot the man in the lower back and pelvis area several times, trying to avoid the body armor. The man immediately fell to the ground as if he just went limp. Damon rushed ahead, kicked his rifle away from him, and pulled his sidearm from his holster.

Jason jumped out of the Toyota and ran over to the first two, verified they were down hard, and yelled, "Clear!"

Damon responded, "Clear here as well, but breathing."

Jason and Damon walked over to the officer that Damon shot as Evan climbed out from under the SUV. Evan collected the first two officers' AR-15s, all of their ammo, and their sidearms. He also removed their radios, thinking they may come in handy in the near future. He then tossed all of it into the back seat of the SUV. He walked over to Damon and Jason, where they watched the downed, but alive, uniformed murderer struggle to breathe.

Jason said, "Leave the bastard here for the kin of those they killed to deal with. He's the one who shot the woman and the old man."

Damon nodded. "Let's take the body armor with us from those two, as well. They may come in handy the way the things are going. This one is covered in blood though," he said, pointing at the dying man.

Evan ran around the house to where Peggy was hiding and

hurried her to the SUV. She stopped in her tracks, in shock at the sight of the downed officers. Evan gave her a tug, pulled her by the hand, and put her in the back seat. Damon and Jason retrieved the dying officer's weapons and ran to the SUV as well.

"Damon, you drive and Jason and I will cover us with the ARs," yelled Evan.

"Shotgun!" shouted Jason as he jumped into the front passenger seat.

"I'll be the trunk monkey, I guess," said Evan. He opened the cargo hatch of the SUV and climbed in to provide cover from the rear. It was then that he noticed the food the officers had seized. "Hey guys, those people died for this food. It should be with their families, not us."

The each silently nodded in agreement. Evan hopped into the back seat with Peggy as Damon turned off the blue lights and drove down the street toward a crowd of people who surrounded the bodies of the victims of the DHS officers.

The people were weeping, with what appeared to be close family members on their knees in emotional agony. When they saw the SUV, some of them ran off thinking the officers had returned, not realizing the gunshots they had heard from down the street was the crew fixing that problem. Damon stopped about fifty yards away so Jason could step out and wave to the people to show them they were not the killers. Once the crowd seemed to understand, Damon continued forward as people came back out into the street.

"Those sons of bitches killed my boy!" an enraged man yelled. "Where are they?" he demanded.

"They are lying in the street a block that way," said Jason as he pointed. "The bastard that pulled the trigger is down there choking on his own blood as we speak."

The angry father and a few other men immediately ran down the street in the direction Jason pointed. Evan popped the cargo hatch and said, "Here is the food they took. It's rightfully yours, so please take it." He then said, "Is anyone here prior service?"

"Two tours in Iraq with the Marines," a man in his late twenties replied. The man pulled up his pant leg to reveal a prosthetic leg with a Marine Corps logo sticker on it. "The second tour didn't work out so well."

"Perfect." He pulled one of the captured rifles and four loaded, thirty-round magazines from the SUV and handed it to the man. "Don't let that crap happen in your neighborhood again," Evan said.

The man took the rifle, looked Evan in the eyes, and said, "As long as I'm breathing it won't. I didn't lose my leg fighting for this country only to come back and have my own government treat my family and my neighbors like this."

"Damn straight!" said Jason.

Evan then took two of the DHS officers' sidearms, gave them to the man, and said, "Give these to people you trust in case you need help." With that, they climbed back into the SUV and drove away.

Damon said, "Okay now. It won't be long before the Feds figure out their guys are down and this truck is missing. For now, though, the markings will give us cover to move freely, relatively speaking, without the choppers calling in an unauthorized vehicle. I'm gonna get us close to the beach but not all the way to the boat. We can't let them find the truck at the pier and put two and two together. It'll be impossible to outrun helicopters in a big, slow boat." He took a quick look at his map and headed for the water.

Along the way, they saw people scatter when they approached. "Looks like people have already figured out martial law isn't a good thing with power-hungry, armed thugs enjoying the power trip," said Jason. "Hopefully, the Oath Keepers won't put up with that crap and will either walk off the job or will deal with the power-hungry from the inside," he added.

"Oath Keepers?" queried Peggy, speaking for the first time since the guys took down the officers who were abusing the citizens.

"The Oath Keepers are active, reserve, retired, and former military and law enforcement personnel who have made a pact to keep their oath to support and defend the Constitution, against all enemies foreign AND domestic—with an emphasis on domestic.

They vow to never go against the people by following the unjust and unconstitutional orders of someone above them, including the president," answered Jason.

Evan added, "The problem is that this administration has been purging the military and federal agency leadership ranks of anyone who displays any loyalties that don't coincide with their objectives."

Damon looked at his map and said, "The next street up will be a good place to ditch this truck. I think we should park it and head off in the wrong direction for a few blocks, then double back to the beach. We don't want someone selling us out and sending them toward Rockaway Point after us."

Everyone agreed and Damon proceeded to Empire Avenue and took another left onto Beach 9th Street. He pulled over and positioned the truck underneath and next to a cluster of trees.

Evan then said, "We can't just walk down the street with these AR-15s in plain view. Let's pull the take-down pins and separate the uppers from the lowers so that we can get them into our packs. We can keep our .40s holstered in case we need them, then we can put the ARs back together when we get to the boat."

"Good idea," Jason said, "and Damon can carry the shotgun under his coat since it's short, as well as the extra pistol we took from the murderer."

After they had got their things together, they slipped out of the SUV and resumed their tactical bound with Jason up front and Evan bringing up the rear. Up two blocks, over two blocks, then down four blocks to the water was their route, keeping a careful watch along the way. They finally came upon the shoreline and took cover behind a dumpster to rally and regroup.

Damon said, "Okay, if we follow the shore to the west, we will eventually come to Rockaway Point and the boat. We have two ways, as I see it, that we can do this. We can wait here until the sun goes down and use the cover of darkness to slip down the beach to the boat. However, that gives the feds more time to find the SUV and get on our trail. If not for our run-in earlier, that would be my pick. So considering that, let's go with the second option and move now and handrail the beach, moving quick but cautious. Then we will try and slip onto the boat undetected and rest onboard until dark. I don't want to pull the boat out in broad daylight."

Evan said, "I agree with the latter as well. Also, since this part of town is relatively quiet, let's increase our spacing. A loner, a couple, then another loner may go more unnoticed if they are specifically out looking for a group of four. Damon, why don't you take the lead since you know where you are going? Jason and Peggy, you stay back to where you can just barely keep him in view, and I'll drop back that same distance. We can still help each other out if need be, but we will dramatically change our visual profile that way."

"Roger that," said Jason.

With that being settled, Damon stood up and said, "Well, I had better get moving then."

As they sat behind the dumpster letting Damon get his distance, Jason and Evan both noticed the helicopter traffic in the general area seemed to be increasing. They wondered if that was just a coincidence or if it was a result of their earlier actions. They took a moment to look off in the distance to soak things in. They really had not had a chance to do that since the beginning of their journey. Off to the northwest of their position, they could see billowing clouds of smoke from what appeared to be Manhattan.

Helicopters, mostly of the UH-60 type, were the only thing in the sky. They had not seen any civilian aircraft in the air since everything had started going down. There were several people they could see off in the distance walking down the beach and a few camp fires there, as well. It appeared that people realized the beach is a good way to get around while avoiding the stuff going on in the city. The only sounds were a few gunshots off in the distance and the occasional siren. The typical sounds of the hustle and bustle of the city were simply silent.

When Damon got far enough down the road that paralleled the beach and appeared to be a man traveling alone, Jason took Peggy by the hand and said, "C'mon, dear; time to look like a couple out for a lazy post-apocalyptic stroll."

She smiled for the first time all day at Jason's odd humor. Jason led her down the street, trying to keep the pace that Damon was setting. Once they were nearly out of sight, Evan scanned the area one more time before leaving the shelter of the dumpsters to keep up the rear. He felt odd not being able to see Damon off in the distance, but was sure if anything happened up ahead he would see a reaction from Jason.

Only a few steps away from the dumpster, two UH-60 Blackhawks came roaring overhead at rooftop level. He could see door gunners hanging out of the door, ready to rip. His heart skipped a beat, expecting them to start firing on him at any second, but they just kept on blasting by. The Blackhawks stopped and hovered over the area where they ditched the SUV. *Oh hell*, he thought. *Here we go.* He quickened his pace and moved closer to the houses in order to try to remain concealed from the view of the choppers as he picked up the pace. He figured it wouldn't be long before the Blackhawk crews realized the SUV was abandoned and would be calling in some of their comrades to scour the area. If that happened, having DHS AR-15s in their packs would be hard to talk their way out of.

After about a half hour, Jason and Peggy rounded the corner and could see some boats moored out at buoys and others tied up at the dock. They saw Damon kicking the sand with what appeared to be frustration. Jason and Peggy made it to him and could hear profanities streaming from his mouth.

"Hey, hey, hey!" Jason said. "What's wrong?"

"Well, the damn boat is here. That's it out there, the *Mother Washington*. The problem is, it's moored out there at a buoy and not at the dock. I guess in my mind, I just assumed it would be dockside. You two head over there by that gazebo and lie low until Evan catches up. I'll flag him down and bring him over, then we will figure this out."

"Roger that," Jason replied as he led Peggy to the gazebo.

As Evan rounded the bend, Damon signaled him to head to the

gazebo. Underneath the gazebo was a three-foot high space from the sand of the beach to the bottom of the gazebo floor. It was surrounded by painted decorative lattice. The Yacht Club had apparently been using this space for beach umbrella storage, as it was now the off season. The space was perfect for the crew. They could hide underneath the gazebo behind the piles of umbrellas while they figured out how to handle their latest hurdle.

As Evan approached the gazebo, Jason opened the hinged piece of lattice that they had been using as the entrance to the underneath storage area and motioned for Evan to come on in. Once inside, Damon caught Evan up on the situation regarding the boat's moorage. Evan shared with them what he saw happening back at the SUV. Just then, two DHS MRAPS sped down the street in the direction of the SUV while two additional helicopters seemed to be joining the search from above.

"Well, they've found their friends, I guess," said Jason.

"Yep, I think at this point we need to lie low here until nightfall, then figure a way out to the boat under the cover of darkness. We would be sitting ducks trying to take a raft or boat out to the *Mother Washington* in broad daylight in the middle of our very own manhunt," said Evan with a crooked smile.

Peggy said, "Man, oh man, what did I get myself into you with guys?"

"Well, you could be over there in the middle of that smoldering mess called Manhattan with Glen right now, or back at the hotel with the people who kicked our door off its hinges, but I don't think you would be better off," snarled Jason.

She just put her head down into her hands and started to cry.

"I'm sorry, Peggy," he said. "I'm just a very to-the-point person when in the middle of a crisis or stressful situation. I guess I got that from the Army, but trust me, having your game face on is how you make it through things like this. There will be plenty of time for decompressing and just letting it all out later."

"Well, guys, let's get some rest," Evan said in an attempt to change the subject. "We've been going non-stop and we need to take advantage of this opportunity to take a break. I'll take the first watch. Jason, I'll wake you up in a few hours and we will go from there." With a nod to the affirmative Jason lay back and put his hat over his eyes. Peggy curled up into the fetal position, Damon rolled over onto an umbrella and in no time, all three were sound asleep.

Chapter 8: Intrusions

Back in Tennessee, Molly was busy managing the kids and trying to keep life for them as normal as possible. With the diesel generator running on demand, most of their daily lives remained unchanged, with the exception of the lack of contact with the outside world. She kept busy taking care of the animals and tending to chores around the house.

A large collection of DVDs kept life for Lilly fairly normal as she was able to keep to the routine of watching her morning cartoons. Molly ran the generator during the day to keep the deep freezers from thawing and to keep the batteries charged. Then at night she shut it off and relied on the twelve-volt DC lights that Evan installed, which were charged during the day by the generator. The twelve-volt DC-powered lights were designed for use in a houseboat or motor home, which made them easy to adapt for emergency in-house use.

After a full day of no power, phone, internet, or satellite TV, Molly pulled Jake aside and said, "Son, you know how your dad is always talking about preparing for things like disasters and stuff?"

"Yeah," he said, not being much for words.

"Well," she said taking a deep breath, "I'm not sure what's going on, but I think we are about to be very thankful for what he has set up for us around here. I don't want to venture out away from the home just yet. We have everything we need here, so there is no reason to take the risk. I'm so busy with the girls, I would like you to be my security guard. Here is one of your dad's .45s, along with three magazines."

She handed him a small camouflage utility bag with a shoulder strap. He unzipped it and looked inside, taking note of the familiar contents. "I want you to keep this with you at all times. You know how to use it—heck, you've shot thousands of rounds through it at the IDPA matches, so just keep it with you. If anything happens, you're my bodyguard, okay?"

"Okay," he said with a proud but worried smile.

"Okay, then. Jake, grab your bag and let's go check on the chickens," Molly said, wanting to keep him busy.

"Okay, Mom," he replied as he grabbed his bag and walked out to the chicken coop with her and the girls.

Molly carried Sammy in a baby carrier sling that held her tightly to her chest, facing forward. Sammy loved being able to see up close everything that her mom was doing while she carried her around. Lilly, on the other hand, being two years old, was quite the little helper. She had to have a hand in everything her mom did. She would reach in and pick up the freshly laid egg and place it gently in the basket with a big smile on her face and say, "Hereyago, Mommy."

After they had finished tending to the animals, they all walked back toward the house together. Molly carried Sammy, and Jake led his little sister, Lilly by the hand. About halfway to the house, they heard the rumble of an engine and the crunch of the fresh gravel that covered their driveway as an old, full-sized Chevy van crept around the corner. It stopped off in the distance, turned its lights off, and kept its engine running at idle. The shadows from the trees kept it dark inside the van, making it impossible for them to see who or how many people were inside. After a few moments, the van backed out of the driveway until it was out of sight and they could no longer hear it.

"Jake, put your holster on and walk out there and close the gate across the road and lock it, then come straight back," Molly said in a serious tone.

He pulled the Kimber 1911 out of the bag and slid the paddle holster down into his waistband, locking it securely in place. He then walked down the driveway, moving slowly so he could hear as he went. He listened closely for voices or the sound of the van. Off in the distance, he could hear the van driving away on the main road. He picked up his pace and hurried to the gate, locked it, then rushed back to the house. "I think they're gone," he said. "Who were they?"

"I don't know, Son, but I didn't like that they seemed to be checking the place out from a distance. We just need to make sure we lock everything up tight tonight, as well as have all of the security cameras and alarm sensors up and running," replied Molly.

Later that evening, Molly was cooking dinner and entertaining the girls when the alarm system, which was powered by the DC batteries, gave the alert tone. Jake ran over to the control panel and said, "Mom! Front gate again."

A motion sensor located near the front driveway gate had detected movement and triggered the alarm. Molly ran to a front window and saw the same van parked in the shadows. Its lights were off and it sat there with the engine idling in the dark, just as before. Molly grabbed the Mossberg 590 twelve-gauge pump shotgun out of the three-gun security cabinet that Evan had installed in the kitchen pantry. It was hard to see the details of the van's occupants due to the failing light of the evening, but she could see the occasional reflection of light from one of the men who had stepped out of the van.

"I think he is glassing us," she said, borrowing the hunting term for using binoculars or a spotting scope. "Well, I'm gonna show them we aren't gonna be friendly. Watch your sisters."

Molly turned the light off in the room in order to hide her silhouette. She slid the window open and fired a shot in the general direction of the van; she then racked another shell into the chamber and fired a second shot. She stepped away from the window and listened. "Wow, that was loud," she mumbled, having never fired a gun indoors before. Although her ears were ringing, she heard the van's doors slam shut as it backed out of the driveway, throwing gravel from its frantically spinning tires.

She went back to the kitchen where Jake was trying to calm the crying girls. They were both startled by the shotgun blasts and could sense something was wrong. "Did you shoot them?" asked Jake in a frantic manner.

"No, that buckshot would barely reach them from here. I just fired a few shots to let them know that if they were up to no good, this house wasn't going to be easy."

"Who were they?" he asked again.

"My guess is some low life is looking for easy prey to loot and rob. With the power and communications down, a lot of people will be easy pick'ns, but not us. Now, while I finish dinner, you go around the house and close and lock all of the security shutters. And don't forget to take your gun. When you get done, we will eat."

Jake ran throughout the house, closing all the reinforced shutters and double-checking all the locks on all the doors. He kept one hand on his Kimber .45 as he made his way to each of the windows and doors. All of this was getting way too real, way too quickly.

That night after dinner, they put the girls to bed. Then Molly and Jake turned on the HAM radio and sat there, listening to the static. *Where are you, Evan?* she thought. *We need you here.* She and Jake cuddled up on the couch as they listened, hoping and praying to hear something from Evan, or just something from anyone out there who could tell them what was going on.

As the morning sun began to peek through the cracks in the shutters, Molly awoke to realize she and Jake had fallen asleep to the soft sound of the radio static. She nudged him awake and said, "Rise and shine, messy head." He rose his head to look at her with one eye open and his hair a matted down mess.

After the events of the previous night, Molly wanted to cook the kids a good breakfast and try to make things seem as normal as she could. She opened the kitchen shutters to let the sunlight in and fired up the generator to get things going. She put some biscuits in the oven and began to fry up some bacon and eggs. *Bacon makes everything better*, she thought jokingly to herself. Just as she started to crack open the first egg, she heard the alert tone from the alarm system again.

"Mom! Front gate again!" yelled Jake.

"Get your sisters," she replied instantly as she grabbed the shotgun and headed for the front window. She felt her stomach twist into knots from the stress and fear of getting into an altercation. She peeked through the cross cutout in one of the shutters and saw a familiar Ford F150 with a Jeep Cherokee behind it, both of which were loaded down with luggage and supplies. A man stepped out of the pickup and waved toward the house.

"It's the Vandergriffs!" she yelled with excitement. "Stay with your sisters; I'm going to go let them in." She threw on her shoes, grabbed her jacket, and headed out the door. She ran to the gate, unlocked it and gave the man a big hug. "Oh, thank God you're here! Come on in. You're just in time for breakfast."

Chapter 9: Reinforcements

No matter how much planning and prepping Jason and Evan accomplished at their respective homes, they still had several great hurdles. The first and most common hurdle shared with other preppers was their distance from each other. At over four hundred miles away, a lot of risks would be taken just accomplishing the linkup between the two families. With this in mind, they knew they had to enlist other families into their plans to make it work. In the event the Jones family needed support during their journey south, Evan couldn't simply leave his own family to fend for themselves, especially with two small children, while he took an uncertain journey to help.

Luckily, like-minded individuals tend to gravitate toward one another. Over the past year, Evan had been building a relationship with an old acquaintance from his Navy days. Mike Vandergriff, or simply "Griff," as most people called him, was a Marine Corps veteran who had served as a sergeant on board the USS *Enterprise* as part of the ship's Marine Security Detachment (MARDET). MARDET's primary mission was to be the physical security for the ship's nuclear arsenal. Evan and Griff had both served on board the *Enterprise* during a deployment to the Middle East shortly after the Gulf War. They met merely by chance, but it was an encounter that would change both of their lives.

At the time, Evan was a young petty officer first class serving as the command career counselor for the EA-6B Prowler squadron that was embarked with the Carrier Air Wing on board the *Enterprise*. During a port visit to Antalya, Turkey, Evan lead a small group assigned to shore patrol duties that patrolled an area not far from the liberty boats that were chartered to take sailors back and forth to the ship. Aircraft carriers are very rarely moored pier-side when making a port call overseas, as the ship is either too large or the host nation simply wants to keep a safe distance from the ship's nuclear reactors. In cases like this, the ship is anchored out in the harbor with a ferry boat service charted to provide shuttle service to and from shore.

While patrolling on a rather run-down street where there seemed to be a dive bar scene of sorts, Evan heard a commotion up ahead and decided to investigate. As his shore patrol team approached the source of the commotion, he found a young American in his twenties swinging fists wildly, fighting off two local Turkish police officers. It looked as if the shore patrol had missed most of the action; there were a few locals who looked like they had been pummeled by a small army and were trying to regain their composure. Tables and chairs were strewn about and broken glass covered the floor and the doorway leading out to the alley. Although the young American was in civilian clothes, his haircut was a dead giveaway that he was from the ship and more than likely a Marine.

Evan quickly intervened and yelled in a commanding voice, "Marine! Stand Down!" He knew that recognizing the man as a Marine may catch him off guard and get him to comply. Marines are well-trained and disciplined, with a heavy respect for the chain of command. However, a few hard drinks mixed with adrenaline can take the commonsense out of anyone, so he didn't want the situation to escalate with the police. Evan calmed the situation down by putting himself on as being much more important than he actually was with the police officers.

A lot of confidence goes a long way in a situation where those involved aren't sure who they are dealing with. Even though the Turkish police officers spoke little English, Evan was able to get the point across to them that he was a military police officer and that in his custody, this belligerent American would be punished much more severely than the mere drunk and disorderly charges they would be pursuing. In an effort to avoid any sort of political confrontation with higher-ups in the police department and the Navy, the officers reluctantly turned custody of the young American over to Evan.

The young American turned out to, indeed, be from the ship.

He was Marine Sergeant Mike Vandergriff. On the way back to the ship, Sergeant Vandergriff, who insisted on being called Griff, explained the story to Evan about how he had gotten jumped in the alley.

He said, "Thanks, man. That was on its way to being a real shit storm back there. I was just going out for a few beers to decompress after getting a Dear John letter from my girlfriend. We were supposed to get married after this deployment, but now she's leaving me for some college douche who's an assistant manager where she works. Anyway, I was on my way to get some love from some hops and barley when those local punks must have thought they had an easy victim."

Evan chuckled and said, "Yeah, what they thought was a lone sailor from the ship was really a Marine with his two best friends, anger, and rage."

Griff laughed and said, "Yep, I introduced them."

Evan laughed and then Griff went on explain that he took on five attackers and was about to take on the police who were called by the bar owner. They naturally sided with their fellow Turks and blamed him for the brawl.

When they got back to the ship, Evan and Griff shook hands, and as he was walking away, Griff turned around and said, "Oh hey, I owe you a beer."

Evan smiled and said, "I'll take you up on that if I see you when I'm off duty."

With that, Evan and Griff went their separate ways, not to see each other again, other than in random passing while aboard the ship, until years later.

One day, while shooting in an IDPA pistol match at the local sportsman's club in Oak Ridge, Tennessee, Evan and Griff were assigned to the same shooting squad. The two men immediately recognized each other and couldn't believe just how small the world was. Back in their military days, when they had met by chance, they had no idea they were both from East Tennessee. Some things just seem meant to happen, they both thought.

Over the next year, Evan and Griff became good friends. They also shared similar concerns for the state of their country and the world, just as Evan and Jason had. Griff, who was now married and lived with his wife, Judy, and his nineteen-year-old stepson, Greg, had begun prepping as well. Given their friendship and common interests, it was only natural that the two families link up. The Bairds, knowing that they would need help in a SHTF scenario, especially before the Jones family arrived, brought the Vandergriffs into the mix.

Evan and Molly invited Griff and family over for grill-out nights on a regular basis. Evan and Griff would use these opportunities to go over possible defensive strategies for the Baird's property. They had planned to have the Vandergriffs meet up with them on the Homefront in the event of some sort of a crisis, as Griff and his wife lived in a suburban Knoxville neighborhood that wasn't at all defendable. Evan had eventually planned to get the Jones family down to the property for a visit at the same time as the Vandergriffs. That way everyone could meet and greet since the three families were now a part of the same team, so to speak. Up to this point though, scheduling just hadn't worked out. Having an airline career and a life seemed to be two conflicting concepts at times. Evan wasn't worried though; Jason and Griff were cut from the same hardcore cloth. These were two men he definitely wanted on his team. In the event of a SHTF scenario, once all three families were together, security watches and a regular division of duties could be established to keep the property running as a life-sustaining homestead for as long as need be.

Chapter 10: A Time for Action

As Evan stood watch while the others slept, he sat there thinking of home. He looked through the lattice surrounding the pavilion up at the night's sky out over the Atlantic. He wondered if Molly was perhaps looking at the same sky, wondering where and how he was in all of this mess. Evan had truly found his soul mate in Molly and knew he could never forgive himself if something happened to her while he was away. He also knew that behind Jason's sometimes harsh persona, deep inside, he felt the same way about his wife and kids back home. That's one of the things that helped Evan and Jason have total trust and faith in each other. They both knew that family would always come before anything else with one another and no outside force could steer them off course.

After about a half hour of relative calm, other than the sounds off in the distance of mayhem reigning through parts of the city, a pair of DHS MRAPs drove down the beach, shining their spotlights in all directions in what appeared to be a very deliberate search pattern. *Oh great*, Evan thought, *they are looking for us, or rather the people who brought justice to their murderous brethren.* Evan carefully nudged the others awake and signaled for them to remain silent and to look and listen. The lead MRAP came to a stop just twenty feet ahead of them. Two officers dressed in full SWAT gear exited the rear of the vehicle and slowly advanced toward the gazebo with their AR-15s at the ready. They clearly were not there for a general patrol; they were hunting.

Jason very carefully whispered to Evan, "If we fire on these two, the gun on top of the MRAP will shred this thing apart. Not to mention the other goons inside with perfect protection from our pissy little 5.56s and .40s," referring to their commandeered rifles and their own service pistols.

"Yeah, you're right. Those poor bastards don't stand a chance," he said with a smirk on his face.

Jason smiled and nodded in the affirmative. As they both reached for the safety selectors on their AR-15s, they heard gunshots off in the distance being fired at a pretty rapid pace, followed by what could possibly be return fire. The officers paused upon hearing the same rifle reports and just then, a frantic call came over the radios they were carrying on their tactical vests.

"Man down! Man down! Shots fired from armed insurgents at the intersection of Beach 9th Street and Lanett Avenue! All units respond! I think we have them!" Without hesitation, the DHS officers ran back to the MRAP and immediately sped away back down the beach.

"Insurgents?" exclaimed Jason with an elevated whisper. "What the heck are they using that term for, so soon after the shit hit the fan? They haven't had time to nail that stuff down."

"Unless, of course, the administration had planned all along to blame any such events on his political, ideological enemies," Damon said. "Blame them for anything that happens and label them as if they are the same ilk as those we fight overseas, and you are well on your way to a successful demonization of your enemy's propaganda campaign. Then you can use whatever means you want to deal with them in the name of national security. In this case, my guess would be Christians, Tea Party groups, NRA members, Constitutional Libertarians, and pretty much anyone else who doesn't toe the line," he said.

"Yeah, the same tactic has been used over and over again throughout history when a dictator or communist/fascist regime needs the general population to tolerate their crackdown on the opposition. This prevents more from supporting or joining the opposition," added Evan.

"Do you think those shots came from the veteran you gave the gun to?" asked Peggy. "I hope those people are okay."

"That seems to be about where we left those folks," replied Jason. "Those folks have to defend their homes and families, just like we need to get back to our families to protect them. I think we should make our move now for the boat while the Feds are wrapped up in whatever they have going on over there."

Just then, two Blackhawks flew overhead at rooftop altitude in the direction of the small arms activity. Damon stood up and said, "Okay, I'm gonna recon the area and find us a way to get out to the boat. I'm not gonna drag it back over here if I find something so keep an eye on me. If I make it to the water with something, I'll cover you while you make your way over to me. The sun will be up soon, so hopefully we can get on the boat unnoticed before sunrise."

"Roger Roger, we'll cover you from here," replied Jason.

As Damon slipped out from underneath the pavilion, Jason took up a position to cover him directly while Evan took up a watch to detect anyone approaching from down the beach. They watched as Damon carefully made his way up to the Yacht Club's main building. He then slipped around the corner where they no longer had him in sight.

After a few minutes without any sign of Damon, Jason said, "I think I need to go give him a hand. You cover me."

"Will do," replied Evan. He then turned to Peggy and said, "Okay, Peggy, I'll cover the building where Damon and Jason are. You keep an eye out for anything on down the beach. We can't afford to be busted at this point." She nodded in the affirmative and took up her position. After just a few minutes, Evan and Peggy heard a noise coming from the direction that Damon and Jason had gone.

"What's going on?" she said.

"Sounds like a small gas engine to me," Evan replied with a curious tone. After a few minutes, it kicked off followed by some banging around and a dragging sound. Just then, from around the corner, came Damon and Jason, side-by-side, dragging a small inflatable dingy.

"Awesome," Evan said with excitement. They patiently waited until Damon and Jason got the raft to the water. Jason took up a cover position with his AR-15 at the ready, and Damon signaled for Evan and Peggy to join up with them. Evan sent Peggy out from the gazebo and covered her from behind. Without saying a word, they each tossed their pack into the raft and climbed aboard. Jason, as the cover man, got in last and gave them a good shove off of the beach.

"Nice paddle," Evan said as he noticed Damon paddling the boat with a plastic garbage can lid.

"Hey, don't laugh," Damon responded with a grin. "This is all we could find. This raft was lying out in that old storage building, deflated. Luckily, there was a gas-powered air compressor out there or it would have been useless to us. It's got a little air leak on the side there, but luckily, Jason, being the Boy Scout type, had a roll of duct tape in his bag. That should hold till we make it out there."

"Don't worry," added Jason. "That's speed tape. If it works on the side of a jet going five hundred miles per hour, it will work on a raft going three miles per hour."

Evan then relieved Damon of the paddling duties and after about another ten minutes, they reached the *Mother Washington*. Evan reached out and grabbed the swim platform on the back of the boat and held the raft in place while the others climbed aboard. After the last one was on, he tossed the trash can lid like a Frisbee and pulled the air plug on the raft to deflate it and dragged it onboard.

"We don't want this thing floating back to the beach and giving someone a clue," he said as he pulled it into the main salon area.

Jason looked at Damon and said, "Arg, what be ye orders thar Cap'n."

"Well," Damon responded with a chuckle, "I want to idle out of here quietly and under the cover of darkness. It's almost sunrise now, and it will take me a while to go through everything and make sure it's ready to travel. Let's all get some much-needed rest today, and we will slip out tonight after sunset. Our trail will be a little colder by then as well. Surely their attention will be on some other insurgents, as they call us, by then. Peggy, you take the master stateroom, I'll take the dinette in the kitchen, as it converts to a small bed, and Evan and Jason can fight over the V-berth up front versus the couch in the salon."

"I'll take the couch. I'm used to sleeping there every time Molly gets mad at me, anyway," Evan joked.

Damon walked over to the starboard side of the main salon, opened a panel, and flipped a few switches. "Okay," he said. "I've got the battery master on for the house batteries as well as the water pump so that the sinks and head... uh, the toilet will work. Just don't flip on any lights unless it's a life or death emergency. We need to practice light discipline because we don't want anyone to know we are on here. The skylights will provide enough light once the sun comes up anyway."

"Aye Aye, Cap'n," they all said with a laugh and off to their respective beds, they went. Sleep is something they all desperately needed after the events of the past few days.

Chapter 11: By the Sea

Molly was making coffee and cooking breakfast while Evan enjoyed lying in bed after a hard day's work on the Homefront. He had just finished building a new chicken coop to accommodate their growing flock. He could hear the kids playing in the other room as the sun began to creep in through the cracks in the curtains. *Well, I guess it's time to get up*, he thought to himself. He threw his leg over the edge of the bed and was startled to see Damon standing there in the galley, sipping a cup of coffee.

"Damn it!" he said.

"What's wrong, Evan?" questioned Damon.

"Oh... I thought you were my wife making breakfast," said Evan in a deflated tone.

"Hell, I thought you'd have better taste than that to be able to mistake me for her," Damon said as he chuckled to himself.

"No, no... I was just having the best dream of being home with my family, is all. But here I am. Dang, I must have slept like a rock." He scratched his head and put his ball cap back on.

"The ocean will rock you to sleep like the best mother, not to mention the fact that you hadn't slept in days," replied Damon.

"Well, either way, I'd love a cup of coffee," Evan said as he stood to stretch.

"Yeah, I didn't want to fire up the diesel generator because it would just draw attention to us, but I happened to remember this stovetop is dual use.

It has electric burner elements, but also has alcohol burners in the center of each element for rainy days... or the end of the world as we know it. It works for either." They shared a laugh as Damon poured Evan a cup of fresh hot coffee.

Just then, Jason crawled out of the forward V-berth and came into the galley and proclaimed, "Oh, hell yes! Coffee!" Damon handed him a freshly poured cup.

"Ahhhh, a remnant of civilization," he said as he took a sip.

"Sorry, there are no bacon and eggs, but there was some instant oatmeal in the pantry. I whipped a batch up for breakfast... or dinner, whatever you want to call this. It's in that pot on the stove and the bowls are in the cupboard. You fellows help yourselves," Damon said.

"So how long have you been up and about?" asked Evan.

"Oh, a couple of hours," he replied. "I wanted to get all of the loose ends tied up long before sunset."

"Damn, it's three o'clock," said Jason, looking at his watch.

"Yep, I'm surprised no one heard you guys snoring all the way from the shore," he said with a grin. "Everything looks ready to go, except for fuel. This thing has always had sticky fuel gauges, so I need to stick the tanks to get a reliable reading. The tanks are under sleeping beauty's bed in the back. The last thing we want to do is head out too hastily, run out of fuel, and end up adrift at sea."

Evan walked over to the back of the salon, where the door to Peggy's sleeping quarters was, and knocked lightly.

"Just a minute," she said followed shortly by her coming up the short flight of stairs into the salon.

Peggy was delightfully surprised to see a semi-hot meal and coffee awaiting her. After they had exchanged pleasantries, they all ate breakfast while Damon went into the aft stateroom to stick the tanks for fuel. After a few minutes, he returned with a smile and said, "Three-quarters in the port tank and nearly full starboard; that's more than enough. Now all we have to do is wash up and wait for sunset," he said with a spring in his step.

They each took their turns taking a shower. The propane-powered hot water heater provided just enough hot water for each shower, but after what they had been through, any shower at all felt like a luxury. That evening, they all gathered in the salon, avoiding the weather decks so as not to be seen and watched the sunset while eating what seemed like a gourmet meal of boxed macaroni and cheese, Vienna sausages, and a can of green beans, which were all prepared on the alcohol burners. They enjoyed the day hiding out on the boat as they each knew once they got underway, all bets were off.

After the sun had gone down, Damon said, "Okay, folks, here's the plan. We are gonna just fire up one engine and idle out of here with all lights off around midnight. We will go on a southeasterly heading to clear Long Island as fast as we can, while avoiding the Jersey Shore as well. I've been listening to the common maritime frequencies on the radio, and there isn't much chatter at all. I can't tell if there are any sort of patrol boats like Coast Guard, Navy, or any of the alphabet agencies out there keeping the coast on lockdown. We will have to just play that by ear."

He then walked to the forward v-berth and lifted the cushions to reveal the storage compartments that were located underneath. He pulled out two rolls of canvas that appeared to simply be extra canvas soft top material. He laid them both down on the dinette table and unrolled them to reveal a pair of M1 Garand rifles. One was a 1943 H&R and the other was a Springfield Armory from 1944. Both were in great shape to be old warhorses.

"Here, guys. I'll be at the helm, so you are our defensive team. I'd like one forward and one aft while underway, each with binoculars and a Garand. If we make contact with an unfriendly or unknown, we will try avoidance, but if that doesn't work, those .30-06 Garands will penetrate a boat hull better than those puny 5.56mm ARs. We've also got three ammo cans of pre-loaded Garand clips. Each of you take one of the cans, and we will leave the third amidships for whoever ends up needing it. Peggy, you stay on the flybridge with me so you can help be my eyes and ears, as well as being a runner or messenger between me and our artillery units here. I'll use the lower salon bridge to fire it up and get us out of here, and then I'll transition up to the flybridge once we are safely clear of New York."

Just then, two large explosions, only seconds apart, rocked the city off in the distance. A huge fireball erupted into the sky, lighting up Manhattan Island like it was daylight.

"Dang, what was that?" exclaimed Peggy.

"Could be anything. Could be more hits from whomever, could also be that the city's gas supply may have continued to flow all of this time until it found an ignition source. All I know is, I'm glad we are going the other way," said Damon.

"Dang, it looks like at least half the city is engulfed," added Jason as he looked on in horror at what was becoming of the city that was a former symbol of American greatness.

"Well, guys, let's move. Evan, undo our mooring line as soon as you hear an engine running," ordered Damon.

Following Damon's instructions, Evan ran up on the bow to cast off the mooring line. He stopped momentarily to look off in the distance at the flames devouring the city. He said a silent prayer for those poor souls who may still be on the island, including Glen. He heard the starboard Detroit Diesel roar to life and looked through the front window into the salon bridge to see a thumbs-up from Damon. He cast off the line and felt the *Mother Washington* surge ahead as Damon slipped it into gear. He then climbed down through the forward deck hatch and walked back into the salon through the galley, joining up with the others.

Damon reached out to the console, flipped the port engine to run, hit the start button, and said, "Screw idling out on one engine! That's when I thought it was going to be a quiet night. I'm sure everyone is a little preoccupied right now to be noticing us," he said as he pushed both throttles forward bringing the forty-three foot long boat to life.

As the *Mother Washington* surged forward and gradually came up on plane, Damon flipped on the radar and said, "We sure don't want to run into anyone in the dark at full speed. If anyone else is out here, they are probably running dark as well."

As they sped away and into the darkness of the Atlantic, they could see a few radar returns out on the horizon. Damon made course adjustments as necessary, giving them as much distance on each target as possible. Off in the distance, Peggy saw some blinking lights out over the water paralleling the Jersey shore and coming right at them. She elbowed Damon and said, "What's that coming at us?"

"Aircraft," he said. "Judging from the altitude, I'd guess helicopters." He held his current course in an attempt to avoid provoking a pursuit.

Up on the bow, Evan watched as they approached with his M1 clutched tightly in his hands, knowing that he would most certainly be outgunned in an altercation with a Blackhawk. As the blinking lights reached the *Mother Washington*, they blasted overhead at what seemed like only a few hundred feet and continued toward the burning city.

"Yep, they've got no time for us," Damon said.

Once they were a safe distance out to sea, and the city was just a clump of flickering lights off on the horizon, Damon pulled the power back and the boat settled down into a leisurely ten-knot cruise. He and Peggy left the salon and climbed topside to the flybridge. Once settled in on the flybridge, Damon called for Evan and Jason to join him.

"Okay, guys, we got out of there much easier than I expected. Now the plan is to parallel the coast at least five miles out until we are south of New Jersey, then turn west and head directly for the Delaware Bay. That's where I would expect things to be a little dicier. Surely we aren't the only people to consider the water a safe haven from the mayhem going on ashore. You three go and get some rest while I mind the store for now. If I need you, I'll press this button and a bell will ring in the salon. I can see everything just fine from up here and I'm almost home to my family. Your journey is just beginning. Rest while you can."

"Are you sure you don't want Evan and me taking turns standing watch with you?" Jason asked with concern.

"No thanks, I'll be fine," replied Damon.

With that, Evan, Jason, and Peggy all went downstairs for a nap. Peggy went back to the stateroom while Evan and Jason took their previous bunk positions as well. Jason and Peggy both fell asleep relatively quick, but Evan remained awake and restless, wondering what the next day would bring. The boat ride was going as they had planned to this point; however, once they arrived ashore, they would be facing an entirely new situation. At that point, the entire scenario was uncertain. First and foremost, they would need to try to contact home. Home... oh, how he longed to be home with his beautiful wife and children where he belonged.

As he finally began to drift off to sleep, the bell rang, and he felt the *Mother Washington* make a dramatic turn as it began to accelerate hard. He nearly fell off of the couch from the apparent evasive maneuver. He leaped off the couch and grabbed his Garand as Jason followed closely behind. They ran out of the salon and up to the flybridge.

Evan yelled, "What's going on?"

"A boat closed in on us pretty fast, and he was running dark as well. I turned ninety degrees and opened her up, and they changed course to follow. They are right behind us and gaining. There is no chance a friendly would be behaving like that."

Just then, a spotlight from the pursuing boat illuminated the flybridge of the *Mother Washington* and a flare was fired overhead. A loudspeaker blasted the message, *"Stop! Arreter! Alto! immediately, or you will be fired upon!"* It was still too dark behind them to see more than a shadow of the rapidly approaching vessel, so Damon flipped on the remote controlled spotlight that his brother had installed on the radar mast and spun the light around to illuminate their pursuers. A few rapid fire shots rang out from the other boat that seemed to be intended for the light. Bullets danced off of the radar mast and some hit near the bridge where Damon was operating the boat. Unfortunately, the design of the flybridge being open from the rear gave Damon nowhere to take cover.

Evan dove onto the aft deck and let all eight rounds of his Garand clip fly in the direction of the spotlight. Jason joined in on the volley of suppressing fire, taking cover behind the steps leading up from the salon. Upon Evan's eighth round, his bolt locked back as he heard the ping from his rifle ejecting the empty clip. He slammed another clip into the top of the action, letting the op rod slam forward to re-engage the aggressor. He resumed firing and a blast of fiberglass flew into his face as a round impacted the hull of the *Mother Washington*, just inches from where he was firing from the prone position. Momentarily stunned and feeling pain in his left eye, Evan reopened his right eye to see a figure in a firing position on the bow of the pursuing boat, which was now just twenty yards in trail. Quickly aiming for center mass, he let off a pair of .30-06 shots at the assailant. The first shot tore into his abdomen. The second shot went high as it recovered from recoil and, with the power of the venerable .30-06 at such a close range, took off the left side of the man's head.

Jason continued to fire into the helm of the pursuing vessel, reloading twice before it made an erratic turn, nearly losing control and breaking off the pursuit. Taking advantage of the pause in the attack, Evan felt around on his face to ascertain the extent of his injuries. He felt some minor cuts and lots of fiberglass splinters, but his eye, thankfully, seemed intact. It was still too painful to open at this point, so he just kept it closed and leaped up to check on everyone else.

To his horror, he turned around to see Jason pulling a limp, bloody Damon from his seat at the helm. Evan ran up to the flybridge and pulled the throttles back to idle, then turned to help Jason get Damon to the deck.

"He's been hit in the back at least a couple times," exclaimed Jason. "He's got a lot of frothy blood, so it looks like a lung shot."

Damon's labored breathing gurgled from his wounds and began to slow, and then stopped as his life slipped away from him. In shock from what had just happened, Evan looked around at all of the blood on the bridge and the now lifeless man who had helped get them out of New York. He felt a mixture of heartbroken sadness and rage. He then thought about Peggy and ran down the stairs, through the salon, and into the aft stateroom to find her cowering on the floor, using the bed for cover. While they had been firing at Evan, who was lying just above her on the deck above, they had riddled the back wall of the stateroom with bullets. She was terrified, having been awakened by bullets impacting just above her head.

He knelt down to her and said, "It's okay, it's all over now. They are gone. We shot the hell out of them so I doubt we will be bothered by them anymore."

"Who was it? What did they want? Why the hell were they shooting at us?" she asked frantically.

"I'm not sure. We didn't get to introductions before it hit the fan," replied Evan.

"Is everybody okay?" she asked.

"Jason is fine. Damon... well... he didn't make it. He got hit in the back while trying to get us away from them. He died protecting us," Evan said as a tear rolled down his cheek.

"Oh my God! Oh my God!" she repeated over and over, nearly hyperventilating.

"Just go sit on the couch while Jason and I take care of everything," he said.

She reluctantly complied and Evan rejoined Jason topside.

"Dude, what's wrong with your eye?" Jason said.

"I got some fiberglass shrapnel in it from a close call. I'll live, but it hurts like hell."

"Well, go wash your eye out while I look for a way to take care of Damon," Jason said.

The two men went down into the salon and saw that Peggy was lying on the couch face down, crying intensely. Jason went forward into the v-berth while Evan went to the galley sink to wash out his eye. Peggy looked up to see what Evan was doing and somewhat regained her composure. She got up and walked into the galley to see if she could help.

"Here, let me take a look," she said as tears still rolled down her face. She examined him more closely. "Ouch, that looks painful."

"Oh, I'll be okay," he said. "I just may need a pirate eye patch soon."

"Well, it looks like you have a scratch on your eye and some debris around it, but I don't think any of the fiberglass shards penetrated it." She went to the stateroom, retrieved her bag, and pulled a pair of tweezers from her makeup kit.

"You brought your makeup as a survival item?" Evan questioned with a chuckle.

"Hey, a girl has to have hope," she said. She took the tweezers and picked all of the fiberglass she could get out of his eye and face and then used some alcohol sanitary wipes to clean the wounds. "You'll probably want to cover your eye and keep it closed for a day or two to keep the irritation down to a minimum while it heals, but I think you will be fine," she said as she put her things away.

A few moments later, Jason came out of the v-berth with the two rolls of canvas that Damon's brother had used to conceal the Garands. He said, "Let's get Damon cleaned up. We can use this stuff to wrap him up tight. We've got to figure out a way to get him back to his family. After all he has done for us, we can't leave him behind."

"I agree," said Evan. He tore a t-shirt and began to make a wrap to go around his head and cover his eye. "Let's dig around the boat and look for some registration or something that will have his brother's address on it. We can try to get the boat as close as possible to there and try to find them. We have to let them know how he fell as a hero, saving us from the horrors going on in New York and helping us to get this far."

"Good idea," Jason replied.

The two men headed topside with a bucket of water and some towels. They cleaned Damon's body the best they could and wrapped him tightly in the canvas. They then took his body to the aft stateroom, where Peggy had been sleeping, and placed it on the bed. Evan fired up the auxiliary generator to power the air conditioning unit for the stateroom and turned it on full cold to help preserve him the best they could. The three of them then looked around for papers that may lead them to Damon's family.

Peggy came out of the stateroom and said, "Hey guys, I've got it. I found it in the nightstand drawer by the bed. It looks like the registration for the boat, some insurance paperwork, and some odds and ends."

"Great, what's the city?" replied Evan.

"Delaware City, Delaware. Do you guys know where that is?" Peggy asked.

"It's right here," said Jason, pointing at a chart that Damon had been using. "It looks like we have to go all the way up the Delaware Bay to the confluence of the Delaware River. It's a town on the bank of the river."

"There is a GPS receiver mounted on the flybridge antenna arch, right?" asked Evan.

"That or a big fishfinder," replied Jason.

"A fish finder would be sonar and on the bottom, not on top like radar and GPS. I'll go check," Evan said as he headed topside. Upon reaching the flybridge, Evan was delighted to see a Garmin combination GPS and fish finder. He powered it up, and once it had run its self-tests, he was disappointed to see the message "SEARCHING FOR SATELLITES/RAIM UNAVAILABLE" displayed, with no indication of satellite reception. Jason joined him on the flybridge to see what he had found. Evan pointed at the message on the receiver and said, "Well, so much for that."

"What?" asked Jason as he leaned over to see the message. He read it, sighed, and said, "Well, either things are worse than we know or the government scrambled the GPS signal for defensive or offensive reasons. Either way, it's no good to us. Gotta find it old school, I guess. Better find a sextant and shoot the stars," Jason said with a defeated chuckle.

"Yeah, I'll get right on that," replied Evan. "With all the power being out, it's like having vertigo out here—dark in all directions. Looks like the fire in the city has died down too. That or we've gone farther than we think. We can always take up an easterly heading based on a guesstimate of our position in relation to the bay. Then we can turn the radar gain all the way up to paint the coastline, try to make out the bay, and head for that."

"Sounds like as good a plan as any," said Jason. "It's almost daylight though, and I'm not sure cruising right up the bay in broad daylight is such a good idea."

"Yeah, you're right," Evan said. "Let's set up a four hour rotating watch, idling on one motor just to keep us roughly in position. Then tonight, we can make our break for the coast with plenty of darkness left for cover."

With a nod, both men agreed and went below. They caught Peggy up on everything they had discussed and got her blessing on the new plan. Since Damon was now being kept in the aft stateroom, they relocated Peggy to the v-berth up front and Jason volunteered to take the dinette.

Evan took the first watch, which, luckily, was mostly quiet and uneventful. As the sun came up halfway into his shift, he sat with a cup of hot coffee, looking out at the beautiful, calm ocean. The sun seemed to rise up out of the ocean itself, washing away the horror of the previous night. He thought to himself, *I wonder if my beautiful Molly is watching the sunrise over the trees back in Tennessee right now.* Since Evan had always had a traveling career, they both often looked at the stars, sunrises, and sunsets, hoping the other was sharing the same view at just that moment. It helped them feel closer to one another, even with all the distance between them.

With the captain's chair on the flybridge kicked to the side and his feet up on the rails, Evan raised his mug to take another sip of coffee. Jason emerged from below with a cup in his hand and climbed up to join him.

"Hard at work, I see," joked Jason as he took a sip of coffee himself.

"Yes, just sitting here enjoying the peace and innocence of nature," Evan said.

"You mean the same nature where a pack of wolves takes down the baby animal while the rest of the herd runs for its life? That innocence of nature?" he said with a smirk.

"Well, at least that's the way the world achieves balance," Evan replied. "Innocence doesn't mean without heartache or tragedy. The wolves aren't doing what they do because they seek to hurt or enslave whatever prey they find. It's their role to fill in the world. They are just a dog being a dog."

"I know, I know," Jason said. "Just jerkin your chain."

Evan reached up to take another sip of coffee, and said, "All of the chaos going on just a few miles away on land... all of it... caused by the innate human desire to control each other, take from each other, and hurt each other. The founders are probably rolling over in their graves at the thought of all the public debt, the corrupt politicians, and the morally bankrupt society that has brought the greatest of all human creations to the breaking point—heck, for all we know, it is already broken."

"Yeah, I hate not knowing what's going on out there, especially back home," Jason replied. "We've got to get some comms going with my house and the Homefront soon."

"Speaking of which, where is the closest HAM in our network of friendly contacts?" Evan asked.

"I was just looking at that in my notes before I came up. Harrisburg, PA, is probably our best bet, which is along our direction of travel to Zanesville," Jason replied.

"Well, after we get to Delaware City and get Damon with his family, getting on a HAM needs to be mission number one. We have got to get in touch with the girls and our kids. So barring some other information we gather along the way, I guess the plan is like we always talked about. We will go and round up your family and your bug out gear and head south to the Homefront," Evan said.

"Roger Roger!" Jason replied. "Hey, look at that over there," Jason said as he pointed off to the eastern horizon.

Emerging from the glare of the sunrise off of the water, they could see a boat bearing roughly on their position. Evan sat up in a hurry and fired up the other big diesel, just to be ready to make a run for it or take evasive action, if need be. After their last encounter, they were not going to take any chances. Evan already had his Garand propped up against the helm within arm's reach while Jason ran down to the salon to grab his. Peggy ran upstairs after hearing the other engine fire up to find out what was going on. They were all a little on edge after last night's events, to say the least.

After the left engine warmed up and stabilized, Evan slipped it into gear as well and began to head away from the approaching vessel at ninety degrees to their heading and at about ten knots. "We will go this way for a bit, and if they change course and take up a bearing on us, we will know something is up. If they just pass on by... well, that will be that," Evan said. "But if it all goes to hell again, this is what I want us to do. Peggy, you're gonna have to drive the boat, but I want you to do it from the salon bridge downstairs. It's too undefendable to drive from up here during an encounter. We learned that the hard way last night. You can't see very well over the bow from down there, but we are so far away from land there is nothing to hit. If we start shooting, just push the throttles all the way forward. Stay on that heading for about a minute, then turn right or left about forty-five degrees. Keep repeating those random turns until it's all over. Understand?"

"Yeah, I've got it. So these are throttles too?" she asked, nervously pointing at the two levers to the left of the wheel.

"No, those are the gear shifters for each engine. Forward is obviously forward, straight up and down is neutral, and rearward is reverse. You shouldn't have to worry about that unless you have to stop. These two are the throttles," Evan said as he pointed to the levers to the right of the wheel. "Just push them up and pull them back together. Got it?" Evan asked.

"Yeah, I've got it now," she said.

"Okay, head on down to the controls downstairs in the salon and just be ready to take over if we say so or if you hear shooting.

Evan and Jason then took up defensive positions with their Garands. They also brought their AR-15s into position, in the event it got close quarters and came to that. As the approaching vessel came into better view, Evan said, "Wait, that thing has masts."

"Huh?" Jason said.

"Masts, like in it's a sailboat," Evan added. "I seriously doubt anyone is out on a sailboat, trying to chase down and attack a power boat."

"Still, let's keep our distance," said Jason.

"Oh, I agree."

As they continued to pull away at a ninety degree angle to the approaching vessel, the vessel changed course and was once again on a heading toward the *Mother Washington*.

"Okay, something's up," Jason said.

Just then, they saw a flash of light from the other vessel. Jason and Evan both flinched and yelled, "Go, Go, Go, Peggy!"

Peggy shoved both throttles forward and nearly fell backward from the acceleration generated by the two strong, supercharged Detroit Diesels.

Evan and Jason both prepared to return fire when Jason said, "Wait... no *pop*; that wasn't a shot. That was a signal light, not a muzzle flash."

Evan ran down into the salon so that Peggy could hear him over the roar of the engines and said, "Wait, wait, false alarm. Pull it back to idle. Let's check this out." He went back outside, picked up his binoculars, and tried to get a better view of the sailboat. They continued to flash a light at them in a pattern.

"I think that is SOS," Jason said, remembering back from his Army days.

Evan turned, ran up to the flybridge, and started flipping channels on the maritime radio. He noticed a well-worn and sun faded decal on the side, which read, "USE MARINE VHF RADIO CHANNEL 16 (156.8MHZ) FOR EMERGENCY".

He flipped to channel 16 and heard a woman's voice repeating the call, "Viking cruiser... Viking cruiser... can you hear us?"

Evan responded, "This is the Viking *Mother Washington*. Who is this?"

After a short pause, a frantic response came over the radio. "This is the *Little Angel*; we have a medical emergency onboard and need assistance."

Evan responded, "We don't have any medical personnel on board."

The panic-stricken voice responded, "My husband is having a heart attack. We are on the boat alone and I can't operate this thing well enough by myself to get him to shore. We went out to sea to run from the chaos going on back home, and in a rush, he left his heart medication behind. Please help me get him to land so we can get him help. He is all I have."

Evan could hear the tears in her voice. He turned to Jason. Jason just gave him the nod and Evan replied, "Okay, but I must warn you if this is a trap, we are heavily armed and we will not be victims."

"Please, please just help me. I'll do anything!" she said frantically.

Evan told Jason, "Go tell Peggy I'll take control from up here and for her to stay down there for now just in case."

"Roger that," said Jason.

"Oh, and while you are down there, scour the medicine cabinets for anything that might be useful, like aspirin," Evan added.

"Will do," he replied as he ran down below.

Evan turned the *Mother Washington* into the direction of the sailboat and picked up the speed to about fifteen knots. Jason came back up to the rear deck and took up a defensive position. As they neared the *Little Angel*, all they could see was a slender woman in her mid-sixties. Her face was red from crying and she looked very frantic and distraught. As they approached to within fifty feet, Evan circled the little sail boat. He saw that it had been motoring on a small outboard kicker motor. The sails were in disarray, and he couldn't see any signs of others.

"Look good to you?" he said to Jason. Jason nodded in the affirmative and Evan began to pull up alongside.

Once up alongside and only a few feet away, Evan pulled the transmissions into reverse and then neutral to stop the *Mother Washington's* forward momentum. The light waves of the morning gently bumped the boats together as Jason climbed on board with his hand on his pistol, which he still had holstered at that point. The woman led him into the small cabin. He ran back out, gave the thumbs-up, and then ran back inside to help her. Evan climbed down from the flybridge and threw a mooring line over to the *Little Angel*. He then climbed aboard and tied up to a cleat on the deck so the boats would stay together. He went inside the *Little Angel* and found Jason on his knees checking the man's vital signs.

"We have to get him help ASAP!" Jason shouted.

Evan threw his AR-15 over his shoulder and let it hang from its sling. He reached down and grabbed the man by his feet while Jason picked him up under his arms. They carried him over to the *Mother Washington*, where Peggy was now standing alongside.

"Give us a hand!" Evan shouted as they heaved the man over to the *Mother Washington* between the rolls of a gentle wave.

Peggy helped Jason carry the man onboard while Evan stayed behind to deal with the other boat.

"Go with them," Evan told the woman, pointing toward the *Mother Washington*. He untied all of the sails on the *Little Angel* and dropped them to the deck. He searched and found the longest mooring line onboard, which was roughly thirty feet long, and climbed out onto the pointy bow of the *Little Angel*. He tied the line to the stainless steel tow loop just underneath the bow pulpit. He then untied the mooring line that bound the two boats together and ran back to the stern of the *Mother Washington* with the line in hand. He took the line attached to the sailboat's bow and ran it through the two tow loops on the stern of the *Mother Washington*, located just below the swim platform.

"I sure hope these hold," he mumbled to himself.

Once he had done what he could, Evan climbed back aboard the *Mother Washington* and ran into the salon to find Jason trying to get the man to swallow some crushed up aspirin bits that he found in the stateroom medicine cabinet. Peggy was hugging the woman and trying to calm her down while Jason did what he could.

Evan said, "It looks like you guys have this under control. I guess we are scuttling the *sneak in under cover of darkness plan*. We just have to make a daylight run for it and hope for the best."

"Roger Roger!" said Jason.

Peggy nodded with tears in her eyes as she was immersed in the sadness and the fear of the woman.

Evan then ran back upstairs, laid his AR-15 on the seat next to him with his M1 Garand still leaning on the helm, and shoved the throttles forward. He turned for a westerly heading to get them headed toward land. They were at least several miles out to sea; he wasn't sure exactly how far and hoped they hadn't drifted too much during the night. He looked back to see the sailboat flailing around in the wake of the *Mother Washington* at full power and said aloud, "Whoops, too much!" and backed off on the throttles to find a happy medium between speed and stability. In the back of his mind he thought, *Screw it, I should just cut that thing loose, but, then again, that boat is probably all they have left in the world. If he's gonna make it, they will likely need it to survive. They ran from the land for a reason. If she tells me to cut it loose, I will, but otherwise I'll try and drag it along behind.*

Down in the salon, as Peggy comforted the woman, she asked, "So, what's your name?"

"I'm Judith, and this is my husband, Bill. Judith and Bill Hoskins," the lady responded.

"Where are you from? What happened for you two to be out here?" Peggy asked.

"Well, Bill is a retired Navy Boatswain's Mate, First Class. We had been in the Norfolk area pretty much throughout his entire Navy career. After he retired, we stayed in the area and he took a civil service job on the base working as a building maintenance man. After our kids grew up and left the nest—one joining the Navy himself, being stationed in San Diego, and the other going off to college in Texas—we figured we didn't need the house anymore. It was always Bill's dream to have a boat of our own to travel in our retirement. About two years ago, we sold the house to finance his dream. With the market being down, it wasn't the nest egg that we had hoped it would be.

"We took that money and bought our *Little Angel*. We moved into an apartment, not in the best part of town due to our fixed budget, and put the rest of our time, money, and energy into our boat. It's not quite what he had always wanted, but at least it was ours. We've spent the last two years working on it. Mostly painting and general fixer upper stuff. We hadn't really taken it out other than to try things out. Then, last week I was at home and all of the power went out. My cell phone was dead too. I heard a lot of sirens all around and some helicopters flying overhead as if they were looking for something. Bill came home from work early, practically busting the door to the apartment down and started yelling for me to pack up. After he calmed down, he explained that there had been several mass shootings on base. Some terrorists with fully automatic machine guns had gunned down innocent people all over the base, from the pier to the commissary. He also said that a few car bombs had gone off and that the Navy was evacuating the ships from the pier.

"On his way home, the traffic was madness. There were building fires all throughout the town and the power was down. He said he could hear some explosions off in the distance but didn't know what they were. With all of the uncertainty, we grabbed our things and headed for the marina. On the way there, we got caught up in traffic so bad, due to the subsequent mass panic, that Bill and I just grabbed our bags and walked the last few miles to the marina where our boat was berthed.

"Our plan was to do like the Navy and pull out to sea to let the madness subside while the authorities handled things. Unfortunately, we abandoned the car in such haste that he left the bag behind that had his medication in it. He has been battling heart trouble for a few years now. Once we got out to sea, we rode the current north on what Bill called the North Atlantic Drift. Bill said it was the current that goes from the Gulf up around Florida and pushes up the east coast to Newfoundland and then across the Atlantic. I guess he underestimated its pull because we went to bed that night and woke up a lot further up the coast than we had intended. Then yesterday Bill started not feeling well. He spent most of the day lying in the cabin. I assumed everything was going okay, yet we had drifted even further north while he was resting.

"He had me run the little kicker motor every so often to push us back to the west to keep within range of the coast. We didn't want to end up going too far out to sea and dying of thirst or something. Today, Bill got up to try and help me with a few things and collapsed. I've never been so scared in all of my life. The terror of knowing you may be losing your soul mate and only friend while on a little boat out to sea by yourself, where there is no one around for miles to help you is overwhelming. I prayed and I prayed, 'Oh please, God, deliver me an angel, please help me save my Bill. Please don't leave us out here to die like this.' And then I looked up and saw you on the horizon. I started the little kicker motor up and ran it as hard as it would go to try and catch up with you. You're my angels. God sent you to me."

Peggy wiped the tears from her own eyes, hugged Judith, and said, "You're not alone anymore." The two held each other for a few minutes and then let go as both women tried to regain their composure.

Jason said, "If you ladies can keep an eye on Bill, I'm going to go check on Evan."

Evan turned to see Jason coming up the stairs to the flybridge. Jason shared with him what Judith had told him about what happened back in Norfolk. Evan just shook his head, and said, "How far does all of this go? Who the hell is doing this and who is helping them? There is no way something so widespread could have gone undetected like this. Hell, they are listening to you and me on our cell phones but they can't stop this crap?"

"Maybe they didn't want to stop it," said Jason. "Remember, it is a whole lot easier to rebuild something into what you want after it is ruined than it is to convince people to let you tear it down in the first place."

Evan shook his head again and said, "I miss the good ol' days when conspiracy theories were about aliens in Area 51 and stuff." They both chuckled under their breath and looked ahead.

"The coastline is getting pretty visible now. It must not be too much farther away," said Jason.

"Yeah, we are making good time," Evan replied. "I'm just glad that sailboat is towing as well as it is. I would have been heartbroken to have cut it loose only for you to tell me the story of what that boat means to them. Even if Bill doesn't make it, Judith should be able to barter it for something to help herself out."

After a few more miles, as the coastline began to come into better view, they saw billowing clouds of black smoke. "What do you think that is?" Evan asked Jason.

Jason picked up his binoculars and said, "Looks like some large buildings. Isn't Atlantic City about the only place with buildings that big along this point of the coast?"

"I believe so—if we are where we think we are, that is," replied Evan. "Crank up that radar and let's get a snapshot of the coastline."

Jason turned on the boat's radar, cranked up the radar gain, and adjusted the tilt as it began to show an outline of the coast. He pulled up the chart and compared it to what he saw on the radar display. "Come left about twenty degrees and I think we will be pointing at the bay," directed Jason.

Evan complied and set a course based on Jason's recommendation. About that time, Peggy came up the stairs onto the flybridge and said, "Dang guys, it's cold up here. Do you want some coffee or anything?"

"You know you're not our flight attendant right now; you don't have to wait on us," said Evan with a crooked smile.

"I know. I just needed to step out for a minute and stretch my legs. Judith is down there lying next to Bill, praying for him. He's looking really pale to me, and his breathing is very shallow. I'm no medical person, but I don't feel good about his condition at all."

"Well, Peggy, since you are offering, we'd love some steaming hot coffee. Besides, you had better enjoy that galley while you can because as soon as we get to Damon's brother, we are losing the boat and may even be on foot."

After a few minutes below decks, Peggy returned with a cup of coffee for both Evan and Jason. She also had two rain jackets that she found in the closet down below. "Here, this should at least keep the wind off of you. How much longer do we have?"

"Oh, thanks," Evan said. "I'd guess fifteen or twenty minutes at the most. When we get close to shore, we need to be ready to defend ourselves if need be, but not too obvious in case there is some sort of law enforcement presence."

"We can just put some life jackets or something over our ARs next to us. Not sure we would need the Garands at that point," said Jason.

"I agree. Can you go ahead and get all that setup?" Evan asked.

"Roger that," replied Jason.

With that being decided, Jason got all of their defensive measures in place and went below to the salon to check on the others. He also let them know that they were getting close to the bay and to stay inside until they figure out a safe place to port. Jason then re-joined Evan at the bridge and said, "I guess I'm riding shotgun, or rather, assault rifle."

Evan looked at him and said, "Oh c'mon, don't call an AR that. When a soldier has one, it's a service rifle... when a cop has one, it's a patrol rifle... but if a citizen has one, it's an assault rifle? What the heck? Citizens do a lot less assaulting than the other two aforementioned groups."

"Yeah, yeah... I know, I know," Jason said. "I just wanted to push your buttons."

As they entered the Delaware Bay, Jason took the chart and said, "It looks like most of the coast on both sides is wildlife management area and the like, probably mostly marshy, otherwise they would have built on it. Damon's brother Jim lives in Delaware City, right?"

"Yep," Evan replied.

"Well, considering that, I think we should just press on to Delaware City. It's the first real populated area where we may find Bill some help, and we don't have time to waste chasing maybes," said Jason.

"Sounds like a plan. You just use those binoculars to scan both sides of the bay as best you can, and I will keep us as far from the shore as possible," replied Evan.

"Will do, brother," affirmed Jason.

As they continued into the bay toward the Delaware River, they saw a few small boats, which were mostly staying close to shore, almost seeming to intentionally avoid the *Mother Washington*.

"Maybe they think we are pirates," Jason said.

"Huh?" shrugged Evan.

"Well, we are towing another boat. They may think we plundered it," Jason said, attempting to keep a straight face.

"Well, you may be joking but that probably wouldn't be too crazy of an assumption right now," replied Evan.

Just then, a center console boat of about twenty-five feet in length left an isolated spot along the shore and began to motor toward the *Mother Washington*. "Well, what do we have here?" asked Evan. "We can't take any evasive action or outrun that thing pulling the *Little Angel* along behind, so you're just gonna have to deal with them with your so-called assault rifle there," said Evan.

"You know it!" said Jason as he uncovered his AR-15 and pulled it into view. He stood up and held the rifle at the ready in the direction of the approaching boat. Upon seeing him standing there meaning business, the boat changed course and headed on out of the bay.

"Funny how that works," said Jason.

"Yep," replied Evan. "Everybody is tough until they realize they may die for what they intend to do."

They kept to the center of the bay and reached the confluence of the Delaware River and the bay. Looking at the chart again, Jason said, "As we go up the river, both sides are mostly parks and wildlife refuge. You will see an island in the middle of the river. That will be the Fort Delaware State Park. Delaware City is directly to the left of that. It's a smaller town, so hopefully there won't be as much mayhem going on there."

As they continued up the river, they both wondered what kind of reception they would receive. They were, after all, strangers driving a boat that belongs to a local, and to add to that they have his dead brother on board with only their word as to what had happened.

"Well, there is the island up ahead," said Jason as he pointed.

Evan pulled the power back and brought the *Mother Washington* to a fast idle, and asked, "Where is the marina?"

"It's actually inland a bit, up a small channel. We will be in tight and not defendable at all if we get jumped. We will be at close range from both sides and won't be able to turn around with the *Little Angel* in tow," Jason pointed out.

"Oh well, gotta risk it for Bill," replied Evan.

"Yep," affirmed Jason. "I'm gonna put this back under my coat for now." He opened his raincoat and hid the AR-15 from plain view.

As they approached the channel that led to the marina, a large plywood sign was erected that said, "Go Away! No Moorage! No Fuel! No Services! You Loot We Shoot!" Evan and Jason both read the sign, looked at each other, smiled, and simultaneously said, "Sounds like our kind of people."

They laughed and Evan said, "Oh well, here goes."

He pulled the left engine's transmission into neutral in order to bring the idle speed down a bit. If they had to come to a stop in a hurry, he didn't want the momentum of the *Little Angel* to cause it to collide violently with them. "There we go," Evan said as he pointed to the pier. "Lots of pier space off to the right."

Several men began to gather on the pier. One had what looked like a pump shotgun, another had a bolt action hunting rifle, and a few others could be seen with bats and other makeshift weapons. "No services! Go away!" yelled one of the men. When Jason stood up to explain, the same man raised the shotgun, pointed it squarely at Jason, and repeated his demand.

Jason yelled, "Do you know Jim Rutherford? We have his brother and a very sick man who needs help."

Meanwhile, Evan was trying to negotiate the big *Mother Washington* up alongside the pier with the *Little Angel* in tow, hoping he wouldn't feel Jason's blood splatter all over him at any second.

The men turned and talked amongst themselves for a moment and one yelled back to them, "Who is his brother?"

"Damon Rutherford," Jason responded.

One of the men then took off running up the pier and into town. Another of the men walked down the pier to get a view of the *Mother Washington's* name art.

"I think they are beginning to put things together," said Jason.

"I hope so. I don't want your blood splattered on my jacket today," Evan remarked with a grin.

A long section of unoccupied pier was available, enabling Evan to pull the length of the *Mother Washington* alongside with the *Little Angel* in tow. He got within a few feet, shut the engines off, and glided silently up against the bumpers on the pier. Two of the other men on the pier threw mooring lines around the cleats on the *Mother Washington* and tied it to the pier while another man went back to do the same with the *Little Angel* as it bumped the pier and came to a stop.

With a suspicious and inquisitive tone, the man with the shotgun said, "Who are you and why are you on Jim's boat?"

"I'm Evan Baird and this is Jason Jones," Evan said. "Down below is Peggy Marshal, and the couple who owns the sailboat are Bill and Judith Hoskins. Bill is in really bad shape and needs to see a doctor ASAP. He may be having a heart attack. We met them a few miles out at sea in distress and pulled them here for help. We were on our way to bring Damon to Jim and to bring Jim his boat back."

"What the hell do you mean *bring Damon to Jim*? Where is Damon?" the man said, seeming to get concerned and tense.

"He was shot while sitting on the bridge by a boat that attempted to hijack us out at sea," Evan said as he pointed to the bullet holes on the flybridge. "He didn't make it, and we wanted to get him back to his family, where he belongs."

The man lowered the shotgun and silently said a prayer to himself. He cleared his throat, wiped a tear from his eye, and said in a somber voice, "Where is he?"

"He's in the stateroom, but let's get Bill taken care of first."

"Right, of course," said the man. He turned and yelled to another man, "Get the cart and get it now!"

The man ran off and came back just a few minutes later, driving a propane-powered golf cart style utility vehicle with a small dump bed on the back. The men all hurried down into the salon, picked Bill up, and rushed him onto the pier and into the cart.

"Ma'am, they are going to take your husband to my sister's house just up the street. She's an ER nurse, and she will do everything she can to help. She brought a bunch of emergency supplies home when everything started to go down. You can ride with them." Judith hurried onto the back of the cart, and the men sped away to get Bill to the nurse. "You three come with me. Jim just lives a few blocks up the street. He's gonna want to hear everything you can tell him."

Later that evening, they arrived at Jim Rutherford's home. They exchanged pleasantries and Evan and Jason sat down with him in the living room and broke the news to him about his brother Damon. He was silent as they explained in detail their perilous trip from the hotel, out of the city, and to the *Mother Washington*. Jim's eyes welled up with tears as he listened. They explained every instance of Damon's heroism in detail: how, without him, they wouldn't have made it out of the city, and Bill and Judith would probably still be floating helplessly out at sea because they would have never been there to find them.

They accompanied Jim to the *Mother Washington* and helped him remove Damon's remains. Jim told them that they would have a ceremony for him and get him buried within a day or two and asked Evan, Jason, and Peggy if they could please stay for the service.

"Of course; we wouldn't dream of missing our chance to pay our respects to our friend and hero," Evan said with a tear in his eyes. They then gathered their things from the *Mother Washington* and accompanied Jim back to his home, where they were offered a place to stay.

"The power has been out all week so all of the fresh food is gone," Jim said. "We will probably have to eat what's in the pantry on the boat very soon. Luckily, I kept it fairly well-stocked with emergency items. Please forgive us for the lack of a decent meal tonight."

"Oh, don't worry about feeding us," Jason said. "We've got some tuna and stuff we can eat; we don't want to take your food."

"Nonsense!" replied Jim. "You risked your necks to bring my brother and my boat back. You didn't have to do that so you are welcome to dinner and I insist."

Chapter 12: Friendship through Fate

That night, they had a simple but filling meal of rice that was boiled in a pot on a propane-powered grill in addition to some canned ham. After they all had eaten, Jim took Evan and Jason into the garage while Peggy helped Jim's wife, Lori, clean up after dinner. "So what do you know about what has happened?" Jim asked.

"All we know is that there were some terrorist attacks scattered throughout New York City that pretty much collapsed the city's infrastructure. Manhattan Island seemed to have nearly been burned to the ground from what we saw on our way out." He then went on to explain what Judith had told them about Norfolk and what they had seen of Atlantic City from the boat.

"Well, guys," Jim said, "it's actually a lot worse than just what you saw. I'm with the Civil Air Patrol, and we've got a pretty extensive radio network."

"HAM?" Jason interrupted.

"No, not HAM. HAM is governed by the FCC, but Civil Air Patrol radios are governed by the National Telecommunications and Information Agency (NTIA). CAP uses private DOD frequencies, which can only be used by CAP members. Our radios have a range of one hundred fifty to two hundred and fifty miles, and that is multiplied by a large network of repeaters. We are basically capable of relaying messages coast to coast."

"Anyway, our guys were reporting what they were seeing all across the country. Several major metropolitan areas such as LA, Dallas, Detroit, and Boston, as well as some smaller areas in the Midwest, have had their water supplies poisoned. There have been thousands of people killed and sickened from drinking tap water. Of course that now means bottled water and water purification supplies are life and death issues and are being fought over. Bottled or purified water is the new money in a lot of the country, as people are afraid to drink from the tap.

"Also, nearly every major city has had numerous transportation system bombings, like the subways in NYC and the train lines in Chicago. There have even been Grey Hound buses explode while carrying passengers. There have been mass shootings, by what was described as jihadist type individuals, in schools and shopping malls and other crowded public places. Police departments, fire departments, and hospitals have been bombed or set on fire. Several large airplanes were stolen and used as flying bombs. A Boeing 737 was intentionally crashed into the terminal at the JFK airport, shutting it down. Power plants have been attacked and at a minimum taken offline, however, several major power plants were completely destroyed.

"The coal-fired plants had their coal stores ignited, creating outrageous fires that took the plants down for the long haul. Nearly every oil refinery in the U.S. was hit as well, ranging from harassing attacks to keep employees away, to all-out assaults. Some received only small scale damage, but others were completely destroyed. Basically, every facet of our infrastructure has been hit, and every safety net that we have had in place was damaged. The transportation, energy, fuel, food distribution, financial system... everything... everything has been hit. Gas stations that do still have gas, don't have electricity to pump it, and the ones that have generators are already out from the panic buying, and there won't be any resupply anytime soon. On top of that, the government is reported to have seized a majority of the remaining food and fuel stores to distribute as it sees fit, which will probably just be to itself and its supporters.

"Just think about how bad Katrina was, yet people in nearby cities and states were able to come and help. In this situation, whoever is behind this has made sure that virtually every populated area in the nation has been hit in one way or another, which means that wherever you are, no one is coming to help because they are dealing with their own problems.

"By the second day, the president basically suspended the Constitution and declared martial law, which you guys witnessed.

Even our CAP radio network was ordered off the air in the name of national security. Our fleet is also grounded, as the entire national airspace system has been considered a no-fly zone. This is bad guys... really bad. Our financial system, which was already teetering on the edge, is simply no more. It's not that the stock market has collapsed; based on what you're saying you saw in New York, the stock market was destroyed. As widespread as this is, I just don't see how we can bounce back. Some of the final chatter on the CAP radios before we were shut down was that the government was rounding up opposition groups and labeling them terrorist groups. They were ignoring the fact that most of the reports that came back were that the attacks, at least the ones that were witnessed, were jihadist or military in nature."

Just then, Peggy burst into the garage with tears in her eyes, reflecting the light from the candle she was carrying to light her way in the dark house. "Bill didn't make it," she said. "He was pretty much dead by the time they got to the nurse. Judith is a mess. She's having a nervous breakdown. I'm going to stay with her tonight at the nurse's house because she refuses to leave Bill's side. I will meet you guys back down here in the morning."

"Okay, Peggy, thank you so much for helping her," Evan said. He and Jason both gave Peggy a hug and Evan said, "Be careful tonight; we will see you two in the morning."

"So where is Judith going to go now?" asked Jim. "And what about you guys?"

"Well, our plan is to head west to Ohio to collect Jason's family and bug out vehicle, and then head south to my family's property in Tennessee to weather out the storm," Evan explained.

"Bug out vehicle? Were you guys into that Doomsday show or something?" Jim jokingly asked.

"No, no, we were a little more subdued than that, but now I'm glad we were crazy preppers. Anyway, I don't know what Judith will do. Both of her children are thousands of miles away, and Bill was all she had. That sailboat was basically their retirement plan.

Without him, she really has nothing to fall back on that I know of," said Evan.

"Well, guys, we don't have enough food for ourselves as it is here, or we would love to take her in, but trust me, it's going to get dire around here really soon. I suggest you take her with you," Jim said with a serious look on his face.

"Absolutely!" Jason replied. "She's part of the group now, if she wants to be, as far as we are concerned. Whether or not she follows us all the way to Tennessee is up to her, but she has a place to go if she wants it."

"So, you say you guys are pilots?" asked Jim with a raised eyebrow.

"Yes, sir; why?" responded Evan.

"Well, I may have a proposition for you. Are you familiar with a Maule?"

"The four seat bush planes? Those things are pretty cool. Quick off the ground, too, if I remember correctly," replied Evan with a peaked interest.

Jim replied, "Well, I have a 1980 Maule M-5. It's out of annual and, technically, the engine is a tad over its recommended time before overhaul, but now that the world has fallen apart around us, that doesn't seem to be much of an issue. It's got a strong running engine with an automotive gasoline supplemental type certification. Being able to run pump gas will help a lot with the scarcity of av-gas being what it was, even when things were good. I also had oil samples done on a regular basis, right up to the point where the annual inspection expired. There were no metal deposits or anything indicating an imminent failure. It's got a simple panel, but it all works."

"Anyway, if Judith has no need for that boat without Bill, and if she wants to go with you, I'll trade her the boat for the plane. You guys can fit all four of you and your bags inside and low-level yourselves all the way to Ohio."

"But didn't you say the entire airspace system is a no-fly zone now?" questioned Jason.

"Well yes, technically, but if you fly at the tree tops, stay over the corn fields, and follow the terrain along the way, you should have a fairly radar-free route from here to there. Besides, I've heard of other guys going up in rural areas to survey their surroundings, and they haven't had a problem. The Feds just don't have the manpower right now to chase every little gnat in the sky. And face it, people are getting pretty darn desperate out there right now. I don't think you'd do very well traveling by land," Jim answered.

"Well, that actually might not be a bad way to go. We have to give her a chance to get over this big change in her life, though, before we offer to trade her out of her retirement dream," Evan said.

"What are you going to do with her boat if she says yes?" asked Jason.

"We will load it up with friends and supplies and the *Mother Washington* and *Little Angel* will be our little bug out armada. We are getting the hell out of here and heading for the islands down south. We are way too close to Philadelphia; if we stick around much longer, the people there will be spreading out in desperation, and we will be right in their path. This little town will overrun by next week at the latest."

"Well, this might just be win-win then," said Evan.

"Oh, and one more thing—we desperately need to get to a HAM radio. Jason and I both have HAM setups at home and our wives have always known that if something were to happen while we were away, the plan is for them to listen every morning at nine o'clock and every night at nine o'clock until we make contact."

"Oh," Jim said, "so that's why Jason asked if our radios were HAMs. Our official CAP radios aren't, but we have a HAM guy in the group. He lives just two streets over. I'll take you there in the morning. There is no power on his street, but he can fire up his generator for a few minutes. We will try and have you set up before 9 am."

That night, Evan and Jason stayed with the Rutherford's, in

their extra room. They tossed and turned all night, both excited and fearful about what they may or may not find out on the radio the next morning. Their exhaustion eventually overpowered their nerves, and they were able to get some much-needed rest. When morning finally came, they were awakened to the smell of Cream of Wheat and coffee. They gathered themselves, got dressed, and proceeded to the kitchen, assuming where the food can be found, the people can be as well. As they walked into the kitchen, they found Jim's wife, Lori, cooking breakfast and coffee on an old Coleman camp stove.

Jim saw them enter the room and stood up. "Good morning, gentlemen. The coffee is ready and the food is simple, but it's hot."

"Sorry, guys," Lori said. "It's just Cream of Wheat, no toast or anything; all of the fresh stuff is already gone."

"Oh, don't worry, ma'am. These days any morning you wake up alive to eat breakfast at all makes it a good breakfast," Jason said with a smile.

After they had eaten, Jim said, "Well, gentlemen, I'm sure you want to get a move on so we are at Bruce's place before nine. Lori will be here while we are gone, just in case Peggy and Judith come by. We had better get a move on."

Evan and Jason were both anxious to get going, so the three men set out on foot to Bruce Thomas's place to see about using the HAM radio. "We pretty much walk everywhere right now," Jim said as they walked down the main road in town. "Gas is too hard to come by to burn up going somewhere you can get for free. Most people around here only have what's in their tank, and when it's gone, who knows when there will be a chance to get more."

"I guess America is about to lose a lot of weight then," chuckled Jason.

"And a lot of the population," replied Jim in a somber manner.

A few minutes later, they reached the home of Bruce Thomas and his family. Bruce was a retired school teacher who became interested in the Civil Air Patrol from his HAM radio usage. He wasn't a pilot but figured he could help out with the CAP in the communications field. He had been a loyal CAP member for over eleven years and grew to become a good and trusted friend of Jim Rutherford.

Once inside the home, Jim introduced everyone, and they quickly got down to business. Bruce had heard about them and was excited to be able to help. "Come on in. Please make yourselves at home," Bruce said as he ushered them in the door. "We don't usually have the lights on, but I fired the generator up to get the radio all warmed up for you. It's this way, just down this hall."

As they entered the room, they were impressed by Bruce's radio station as well as the military memorabilia that he had displayed all over the room. "Now, who are we calling first?" asked Bruce.

Jason pulled his small notebook out of his pocket and flipped through the pages to find the frequency he needed in order to contact his wife in Zanesville. "Do you mind if I go first?" Jason said, looking at Evan.

"No man, of course not. Go for it," Evan replied.

Jason sat down at the radio and watched the clock tick by. It was currently 8:55 am, and it seemed like the next five minutes lasted an eternity. At exactly 9:00 am, just as he was about to key up the microphone, he heard, "JJ220... are you there?" It was his wife, Sarah.

Jason stood up from the seat in excitement and grabbed the microphone as he broke down in tears. "Yes, baby, yes, I'm here. Oh, thank God you're there! How are you? How are the kids?"

"Daddy! Daddy! Daddy!" came across the radio next.

Bruce, Jim, and Evan stepped out of the room for a moment to give him some time to talk to his family in private. When they came back in, Jason was all smiles. He said, "Have you heard from Molly?"

"Yes," Sarah said. "We talk every day on here. She contacted me shortly after it all started and we have been keeping each other up-to-date ever since. She said that Griff and his family have joined up with them on the Homefront and that with the extra security they are providing, everything is secure."

Evan wiped a tear of joy from his eyes as he heard the good news. "I owe you the beer now, Griff," he said aloud.

"How are things in Ohio?" Jason asked.

"Not so good. There is no electricity and it's starting to get really cold at night. Crime and looting have been getting worse and worse. From what I hear, the masses are starting to leave Columbus in search of food and water. They are hitting and looting the outlying towns and neighborhoods pretty hard. I've been afraid to drink the water after all that has happened, so the boys and I have been filtering the rain barrel water and using it. We are doing fine, but we really need you get here soon, before the city rats, as Evan so eloquently puts it, make it as far as Zanesville."

"We are working on that, baby; we might be there sooner than you think. I can't give details now, but just know we are on our way. I'm not sure when the next time we can get to a radio will be. Keep checking just in case, but cut your frequency down to just the morning call," Jason said as he wiped another tear from his eyes. "I love you, Sarah! I love you, boys! Take care of Mommy. Daddy will be home soon." With that, he signed off.

After Jason was done, Evan made his call and, right on schedule, Molly was right there waiting. They also shared a special, emotional moment. She let him talk to their kids and then she caught him up on the situation in Tennessee. She explained what had happened prior to the Vandergriffs arriving, and how the extra security had really helped take the burden off of her. Evan then updated her on the fact that they were, indeed, going to retrieve Jason's family from Ohio and would be heading south very soon. After a very emotional few minutes to say goodbye, he signed off as well and regained his composure. "Oh, thank the Lord they are all okay," he said.

They thanked Bruce over and over for letting them use his radio, then Jim, Evan, and Jason got on their way back to Jim's house to see if Peggy and Judith had returned. Evan and Jason both walked with a little extra spring in their steps, knowing that both of their families were doing well.

Upon arriving at the Rutherford home, they found Peggy, Judith, and Lori sitting at the kitchen table having a cup of tea. The mood was somber due to Judith's loss, so Evan and Jason kept their happiness subdued out of respect for Judith. She looked as if she had been up crying all night. Her eyes were swollen and red, but the expression on her face showed that she was trying to be strong and keep herself going.

Before Evan or Jason could say a word, Peggy burst out with, "Judith is coming with us. I told her she can stay with me and Zack when we get to Cincinnati."

With a smile, Evan responded, "Well, that makes it easy then. We were just about to try and convince her to come along."

Judith smiled for the first time since they met her. "I prayed for angels, and oh, how the Lord sent me my angels."

After lunch, Evan and Jason caught Peggy and Judith up on their contact with home and they solidified their plan to head initially for Zanesville and then on to Cincinnati before heading south to Tennessee. Jim took advantage of this moment and made his offer to Judith to trade the airplane for her boat, and she graciously accepted.

"Please, use the boat. Please let it take another family to safety like it delivered me to my angels. I have no doubt that Bill and I would have died in Norfolk if we didn't have our *Little Angel* to whisk us away. And my poor Bill died because of his efforts to get me to safety. Just take good care of her and don't change her name."

"Yes, ma'am. I will take great care of her, and since she will be taking care of us as well, she will be our *Little Angel* too," Jim said as she gave him a warm hug.

The next morning, several dozen people from the town gathered to perform a ceremony for both Damon and Bill. The pastor of the church that the Rutherford family regularly attended presided over the simple, yet fittingly beautiful, ceremony. Judith said her final goodbyes and Evan and Jason both thanked the Rutherford family publicly for having been led out of New York by Damon. To them, he was truly their hero.

The next day, Evan, Jason, Peggy, and Judith gathered their things and began to prepare for the next leg of their journey. Lori gave them each two packets of instant oatmeal and a packet of instant Cream of Wheat and said, "I'm sorry it's not much to help get you on your way, but it's all we can spare. Everything else we have is going on the boats with us."

Peggy and Judith both told her apologizing was nonsense, and that they were thankful to get anything at all. They explained that they felt as if they already owed the Rutherford family a debt that they could never repay, and that they appreciated all of the help they had received.

Jim looked at Evan and Jason. "The plane is out at a little make-shift grass strip at a friend's farm. It's only about a thousand feet long, but the Maule is good for that."

"Are there any trees or obstacles at the end?" asked Evan.

"No, just a fence. There are some trees along the side, but nothing to worry about," he replied. "We will need to drive out to the farm. It's about twenty miles from here, so it's a little out of our walking range. We can take my crew cab F250 pickup. Your bags can go in the back, and we will all fit up front. You guys need to be armed up, though. We may have our little town fairly secure, as the townsmen have banded together to do security patrols..."

"You mean like the gentlemen that met us at the pier?" Jason interrupted with a crooked smile.

"Yes, exactly," Jim continued, "but once we get out of our own little world, the people venturing out of Wilmington may get in the way. They may see that we have gas and get a little grabby. Fuel is food right now. You can run a vehicle to go find food, and then you can run a generator with it to cook the food."

Evan looked at Jim with a concerned face. "Taking us out there isn't going to burn too deep into your fuel supplies, is it?"

"No, not at all," Jim replied. "I have a few fifty-five gallon drums of stabilized, high octane and a hand pump in the barn with the plane. I had to be my own fuel supplier, operating the plane out of a farm. The Maule should be full of fuel already. We kept it topped off to keep moisture from condensing in the tanks. Ice in your fuel is a problem you need to keep an eye on, running pump gas in your bird. So much of the pump gas these days has ethanol in it, which attracts moisture.

"Damn government requirements," he mumbled, getting sidetracked. "Anyway, I'm gonna bring the barrels back with me and we are going to load them up and take them with us. The *Mother Washington* runs on diesel, of course, but the kicker motor on the *Little Angel* is gas so it may come in handy. Carl, here, is going to ride out there with us to help me with the barrels and to ride shotgun on the way back," he added.

Carl was a tall, sturdy fellow, about six-and-a-half feet tall, and carrying a Bulgarian AK-74S that was painted woodland camouflage. The tube style side-folding stock was wrapped in olive drab paracord, and it had an EOTech 512 mounted on a receiver mounted, quick-detach rail. He also wore a Glock 35 in a drop-leg holster, which was painted to match his rifle. Evan took a look at Carl, his choice of equipment, and his demeanor and instantly felt Jim was in good hands for his return trip.

They exchanged handshakes and pleasantries with Carl and then loaded their things into the bed of the truck. Carl said, "I'll ride in the back with the gear. That way no one can reach in and swipe anything, not to mention it would be a little tight in the cab with six of us, with Jim's truck being a stick shift and all."

"That sounds good," replied Jim.

They climbed into the cab of Jim's crew cab F250. Jason rode in the shotgun position up front with Jim, Evan rode behind Jim on the driver's side, while Judith sat in between him and Peggy. This gave them rifle coverage on both sides, and Carl could cover the rear from the pickup bed or pop up and cover the front if need be. All the men kept their rifles handy and in plain view to warn anyone who may have nefarious intentions to seek their prey elsewhere.

They were taking only back rural roads to get to the farm as well. This would reduce the chance of having a run-in with any sort of government types.

Once everyone was loaded up, they got on their way. After a few miles, they came across several groups of wandering people carrying signs that were pleading for food and water. "Damn, it's only been a week, and people have already run out of everything and are starving," mumbled Jason.

"Yes, it's sad, really. And over the past few years, the government has been putting people who prepared to be able to feed their own families on watch lists," replied Evan.

Just then, a group of people standing on the side of the road shoved a young boy of around eight or nine years of age out in front of Jim's F250. He slammed on the brakes while screaming a few expletives and narrowly missed hitting the boy. The people then stood around the truck as if they were trying to keep Jim from driving away.

"Give us some food or fuel and we will let you go!" one of the men yelled.

Jason raised his AR-15 and pointed it at the man as Carl popped up on one knee in the bed to cover the rest of the crowd and said in a commanding voice, "Move or die."

"So you're gonna shoot women and children just to get them out of the way over some simple stuff," the man yelled back.

"Nothing simple about survival, my friend. Move your people or I'll smoke you!" Jason ordered.

"Go ahead! I don't want to live in a world where I can't feed my kids!" the man yelled as he reached into his waistband and pulled out a flare gun.

He immediately raised it to Jason's open window as if he was going to fire. Jason didn't hesitate and fired two rounds into the man's chest at nearly point-blank range. To Judith, this being her first armed conflict, it was like it all happened in slow motion. She saw the rounds strike the man's chest and saw the exit wounds spray a mist of blood and particles out of the man's back. As the man fell backward from the impact of the rounds, the flare gun went off, launching a screaming hot flare at the truck window. Luckily, as the man fell backward, the shot went high and grazed off the top of the truck, ricocheting into the air. At the same time, Jim floored the throttle, causing the people blocking their path to dive out of the way.

As they peeled away, Peggy and Judith held each other tight and ducked down into the back seat. Evan and Jason held their rifles at the high ready as Carl maintained a watch on the road behind them, providing cover while Jim drove them to safety.

Once they cleared the area, Jason yelled, "Damn it! Damn it! Damn it! Why the hell did he make me do that?"

In a stern and collected voice, Jim replied, "A lot of these people weren't on their game before all of this started to happen, so they just can't handle it. They have become the bad side of what humanity has to offer. Society has trained the provider out of a lot of men. In my opinion, any man who can't provide for his family— not just in an economic way, but in a physical way, like hunt, fish, or whatever it damn well takes—isn't a man; he is merely an adult male. We've got way too many adult males and not nearly enough men these days."

"Yeah, well, I have a feeling our current state of things may just thin the herd a little," Jason said in disgust.

Evan looked over and tried to reassure Judith that everything was going to be okay. She was cowered down in the middle of the seat, shaking and crying in terror. She was already in an emotionally weakened state after having just lost her husband, and now she had just witnessed her first violent death. It was a lot for her to handle. Peggy simply held her tight to give her support. Evan could tell Peggy had changed quite a bit from the naïve, young woman that she was just a week ago. She was now the rock that Judith needed. Some people rise to the occasion when truly tested, and some people become a burden on those around them. Peggy was doing quite well, and Evan knew that if they were able to reunite her with her son, Zack, that is exactly what he would need.

Chapter 13: Charity

Back in Ohio, things had been relatively uneventful for Sarah and the kids. Jason's foresight and planning had given them all they needed to get by while they awaited his return. Unfortunately, often in the past, when Jason tried to explain certain survival strategies, like operational security and keeping what you have as low profile as possible, she just humored him and basically tuned him out. She respected that he was such a good husband and father; he wanted to be able to protect and provide for his family no matter the scenario. At the time, though, she didn't feel his paranoia about the fragility of society was warranted. Like most Americans, she had been lulled into the false sense of security that bad things happen, but only in other countries.

Unfortunately, she would learn the hard way that Jason's logic and paranoia were correct. After she had made contact with Jason via Bruce's HAM radio, she felt a great sense of relief and happiness. She wanted to celebrate by cooking the boys their favorite meal of cheeseburgers and potato chips. She thawed some hamburger meat from the freezer, which she kept cold by cycling the generator a few hours per day, and fired up the propane grill. Although it was quite chilly out, the boys were in the backyard playing with their dog, Browning, while Sarah cooked. Browning was a mix of Rottweiler and a few other unknown breeds. He looked way more intimidating than he was. He was mostly just a big teddy bear at heart, but he kept a keen eye on Sarah and the boys while Jason was away.

She had just flipped the burgers over and turned to go into the house to get the boys some extra slices of cheese for their super-cheesy cheeseburgers, when she was startled to see one of her neighbors from down the street standing in their backyard, looking at her. "Holy crap, you scared me!" she said as she caught her breath.

It was Brandon Murphy, a thirty-six-year-old real estate agent who hadn't been doing very well during the recent downturn in the economy. When things were booming, his kids went to private school, he and his wife both drove expensive luxury SUVs, and they took expensive vacations on a regular basis. He and his family basically spent every penny he earned, assuming that the U.S. economy would always be fruitful and that they would always have what they wanted. Since the downturn in the economy had been accelerated after the past few elections, yielding more big government socialist policies and killing economic growth, he went from financial bliss to misery. Both of their expensive SUVs were repossessed, their kids were back in the local public school, and their home was put up for sale to avoid foreclosure. All of this stress brought Brandon and his wife to the verge of divorce, as she considered their own personal downturn to be his fault. He simply hadn't worked smart enough or hard enough, in her opinion. He was just a shell of the man that he once was.

After he had startled her, he said, "Smells good, got any extra? With the power being out for so long and not being able to get gas for the cars to try and find food elsewhere, we are running pretty low. You look like you're doing well though."

"We are getting by," she cautiously said.

"So, is your husband out of town?" he asked. "I know he travels for work a lot and I haven't seen him around the neighborhood playing with the boys like he usually is."

She hadn't had a reason to mistrust Brandon in the past, but the entire situation over the past week made her a little more cautious. "Oh, he's fine. He should be home any time now," she said, trying not to give anything away that she didn't have to.

"Well, anyway," he said, "I was just walking around the neighborhood and smelled your delicious burgers there on the grill and thought you may have some extras that maybe I could take back to the wife and kids. We will be able to pay you back, of course, as soon as all of this blows over."

Thinking of how embarrassing it must be for him to have to

walk the neighborhood in search of handouts for his family, she said, "Sure, let me get you something to put them in."

She went into the house for a few moments and came back out with a plastic container to put a few burgers in, as well as a plastic shopping bag with buns and some condiments, just in case they were out of those at his house as well. She looked to where he had been standing before she went in, but he wasn't there. She immediately looked around the yard and saw him talking to her sons while petting Browning on the head.

He appeared to just be acting neighborly to the boys, but for some reason it just didn't feel right. "Here you go, Brandon," she said loudly in order to get his attention. He broke off the conversation with the boys, smiled, and walked back over to the patio. "Here you go. There are four burgers with some fixings for you in the bag. Tell your wife I said hello," she said as she placed the container in the bag with the buns and handed it to him.

He said, "Thanks a lot, and I will. You and your boys have a great day and we really do appreciate it."

As he walked back around the house and down the sidewalk, she called for the boys to come over. They ran over to her and she asked, "What was Mr. Murphy talking about?"

Michael responded, "He was just saying how lucky we were to have so much food and wondered where we got it all with the stores being empty and all."

"Really?" she said. "So what did you tell him?"

"I just told him Daddy has a lot of food for us, and that we will never go hungry thanks to him. Then he asked us where Daddy found the room to keep it all. That's when you came back out. He walked off before I could answer."

Sarah got down on one knee at eye level to the boys and said, "Now, boys, listen to me and listen good. Don't ever, ever tell anyone what we have here at home, especially not now. There are a lot of people out there that would like to take what we have without your father here to keep us safe, so I want the both of you to keep our food and supplies top secret, okay?"

"Okay, Mommy. I'm sorry that I talked to him," he said.

"Don't be sorry, Michael; I should have had this talk with you already. Things just aren't the same right now and we need to be careful," she said as she gave them both a big hug and a kiss. "Okay, boys, let's go in and eat before the burgers get cold." She then led them into the house and locked the door behind her. *I think I have to step up my game around here until Jason gets home*, she thought to herself.

That night, she went around double-checking that all of the doors and windows were closed and locked. She said, "Boys, why don't the two of you sleep in here with Mommy tonight, that way we can snuggle up while I read you a story."

Both boys were excited and grabbed their pillows and ran into their mother's bedroom right behind her. She took out an oil lamp that Jason had placed in the closet for a reading light; he had an oil lamp and matches strategically placed in each room, which was another one of his simple little preps that she was beginning to appreciate. For the first time, she took Jason's .45 caliber Springfield Armory TRP out of the nightstand handgun safe. Her growing uneasiness made her decide that it was now appropriate to keep it handy at all times, especially after being surprised in her backyard by a neighbor that day. She figured that if something like that happened again, and they at least saw her with a gun in her possession, they may think twice about any assumptions they might make. She then read the boys their favorite book and they both fell asleep in her arms. She kissed them each on the head, said a little prayer, and snuggled in beside them for the night.

The next morning, she went out to the backyard to let Browning in, but he wasn't there. "Browning!" she yelled. "Here boy!" Her heart felt heavy, as she knew something had to be wrong. Browning was always waiting happily at the door to be let in first thing in the morning. Their average-sized suburban backyard did not have many places where he could be. She then heard a whimpering coming from the large storage shed in the backyard. She started to walk over to it and remembered to go back in first and grab Jason's gun. She slid the paddle holster into the waistband of her pajamas only to see that the weight of the gun was too much for the elastic band. *Oh well*, she thought to herself, *I'll just carry the thing*.

She walked out to the shed, looking around carefully as she went. She heard Browning whimper and whine again. It sounded like it was coming from underneath the shed, which is where he took regular naps during the day while seeking refuge from the sun. "Hey, buddy, what's wrong? Come on out," she said. He just lay there, breathing heavily with large amounts of drool coming out of his mouth. There was also vomit clinging to his fur around his mouth. "Oh my God, Browning! What's wrong with you?" she said aloud as she reached underneath and slowly pulled him out.

Being of small stature, she knew she couldn't pick the big dog up to carry him back into the house. With that in mind, she went over to the shed to get something to drag him through the grass to the house. As she reached up to the padlock to work the combination, she noticed the screws holding the hinges on, that were normally covered in rust, had been worn shiny and were stripped out. It was obvious that someone tried to take the hinges off with a screwdriver.

Luckily for them, Jason used JB Weld under the screw heads and Gorilla Glue in the holes in the wood to help make their installation a little more tamper-proof. Knowing that someone had been in their yard last night made her heart sink in her chest, and she realized Browning may have been given something to incapacitate him. She rushed to open the lock, and once she got the door open, she pulled out an extra sheet of metal siding that was leftover from building their rabbit shelter, and dragged it over to Browning. She loaded him up and began to pull him to the house, using the metal siding as a sled. She paused and thought, *I had better check on the rabbits, too, while I'm out here*. She jogged over to the rabbit pen and was shocked to see that they were all missing. Someone had taken every last rabbit from the pen.

At this point, her feeling of nervousness turned into rage. She felt as if her family home had been violated. Someone stole from them, someone who knew what they had in the backyard; someone had taken food from her family that Jason had worked hard to put in place. She turned back to Browning, jogged to him, and dragged him to the house. She opened the sliding glass doors on the patio, pulled him inside, and locked them behind her.

The boys, who were at the kitchen table eating oatmeal with dehydrated strawberries, dropped their spoons and ran over to Browning in a panic. "Mommy, Mommy what's wrong with him? Why is he acting like that?" Kevin said with tears in his eyes.

"He's just sick, boys. He must have eaten something bad that he found in the back yard. I'm sure he will be fine. We will just keep him in the house until he gets better," she said, trying to mask her true emotions of fear and rage. *If I find out who did this, they will regret ever stepping foot on this property*, she thought to herself as she looked through the sliding glass door into the yard.

Chapter 14: Faith and Friendship

The rest of the drive to the farm, where the plane was kept, was uneventful, yet tense. They only came across a few more groups of people along the road, in addition to one vehicle that was driving as they were. It was a gray Nissan Pathfinder with four guys who looked like they were straight out of Philly. They definitely didn't look like locals, who were generally the only people who frequented the backroads in the area. Most of the people who used these roads were local family-owned farm workers, which regardless of ethnicity, had a general look about them by the way they dressed as well as the tell-tale signs of working long days outdoors.

As they passed by Jim's F250, uneasy stares from each of the vehicles were the only interactions. As they drove on by, Carl noticed that there was no license plate on the back of the vehicle and the lock on the tailgate hatch was damaged. He knew the odds were that they were up to no good and only hoped they weren't headed back toward Delaware City—at least not until Jim's group got underway and they got out of there.

When they arrived at the gate to the farm, Jim honked the horn three times. Carl jumped out of the back of the truck, walked over to the gate, unlocked the large padlock, swung the gate open, and held it as Jim drove through.

"What was the horn for?" asked Evan.

"Oh, that was just to make sure Charlie isn't surprised to see us driving across the field toward the barn. I don't want him to get trigger happy or anything."

He pulled to a stop just past the gate and waited for Carl to hop back in the bed after closing it again then they proceeded. Jim looked at Jason in the passenger seat and said, "I'll drop you guys off at the barn and you can check the bird out and get her all dusted off. I'll drive back up to the house to explain what's going on to

Charlie, then I'll be back down in a bit."

They pulled up to the barn and everyone got out of the cab of the truck and Carl hopped out of the back. Jim took them over to the main doors where he removed the old rusty lock and chain. He and Carl then swung the barn doors open to let the daylight in. There sat the Maule M5-235C parked diagonally in order to make room for an old Ford tractor and some implements.

"She's a little dusty, but trust me, when we parked her, she ran and flew great. I just got a little busy and the next thing I knew, she was out of her required annual inspection. She's sat for the better part of the last seven or eight months. We may need to put a quick charge on the battery, but other than that, I think you'll be happy with her."

Jason and Evan walked around the plane together and began to go over the details. Jason asked Evan, "Do you have any tail dragger time? I've always been in tri-cycle birds."

"Yeah, I've instructed and flown in quite a few from Citabrias to Stinsons to C-195s. Never a Maule, but it should be pretty straight forward," Evan replied.

"Good," Jason said. "You can do the takeoff and landings then."

They checked the prop and it looked good with no leaks coming from the hub. No leaks were found around any of the seals on the motor either. Jason checked the oil; it was clean and the level was right where it should be.

Jim saw Jason looking at the dipstick and said, "There is a case of Aeroshell oil on that shelf in the back that you are welcome to take with you. I won't have a need for it."

"Thanks," Jason said with a nod.

The panel was a straight forward "six pack", as it is commonly referred to. This meant it consisted of two horizontal rows of three round mechanical instruments. The top row from the left to the right consisted of the airspeed indicator, the attitude indicator, and the altimeter. The bottom row consisted of a turn coordinator with an inclinometer, a heading indicator, and a vertical speed indicator. These basic instruments could be found in most airplanes made before the glass cockpit era that came into play in the mid to late 2000s. Evan and Jason, both being trained on this traditional setup, felt right at home with it. The aircraft was powered by a simple two hundred thirty-five horsepower horizontally opposed, air-cooled, carbureted Lycoming engine.

Jason joked, "And I used to think of that old magneto ignition system as being ancient junk, now I look at it as being EMP proof."

They both shared a chuckle and continued to check out the rest of the airplane. "What's the fuel capacity?" asked Evan.

"Forty gallons at a 12.5 gallon per hour burn. That should give you about three hours and twenty minutes at seventy-five percent power down low. When we bought it, we wanted the sixty-three gallon long-range tanks but got a sweet deal on this one."

"Oh well, forty will do," replied Evan. "It should only be about two and a half hours to Zanesville, so that gets us there with a little to spare."

They checked the flight controls and everything seemed tight. They also checked all of the flight control cables that they had access to. Jason turned to Evan and said, "Looks good to me; how about you?"

"Oh, I love it. You made a great trade, Judith," Evan said as he looked at her and smiled.

"Well, at least I could contribute something," she said.

Jim looked at them and said, "So what's the plan? Are you leaving tonight under the cover of darkness?"

"That would normally be a good idea," Evan replied. "But under the circumstances, with blackouts being the norm, we would have to time it so we arrive after sunrise since there won't be any airport lights operational. That would put us at the risk of morning clouds or fog as well. Not to mention the fact that hugging the terrain at night would be risky, and if we had a problem and had to make an unplanned landing, we would be up the creek without a paddle. With no power on the ground, there are no runway lights or instrument landing systems or the like to get us down without being able to see.

"Also, considering how late it is in the day already, by the time we get the battery charged, I think we will be cutting it too close to getting there in the dark. I think our best bet would be to get it ready, get a good night's sleep here in the barn, if that is okay with Charlie, of course, and head out first thing in the morning. If we buzz the treetops all the way there, by the time anyone sees us, we will be out of their sight in a flash."

"That makes sense, I guess," replied Jim. "If you want to get that old generator over there fired up so you can plug the charger in, I'll drive on up and tell Charlie what we are doing down here and what your plans are. I don't think he will have a problem with that though," said Jim as he walked over and hopped in the truck.

Carl helped Jason and Evan drag out the old generator and get it running. It took quite a few pulls on the recoil starter, but it finally shook, shuddered, and roared to life. They went ahead and practiced a load-out of all of the gear behind the back seat of the Maule.

"It will be a cozy fit, but it will work," Evan said as he scratched his head and put his cap back on, standing back to admire his packing job. "I'm just glad this is the big motor Maule and not the one hundred and eighty horse model, or I would be sweating the grass strip we have to get off of with our load," he added.

"Yep, it's kind of short compared to what we are used to," said Jason.

Evan was flipping through the airplane's pilot operating handbook and other documentation that was in the seat back pocket. He stopped on a page of interest and said, "Well, it says here at max gross weight, we can still get off in six hundred feet. Jim said the strip is around a thousand so we should be fine."

Just then, Jim pulled back up to the barn in his F250 with a grizzled-looking old man with a fuzzy gray beard in the passenger seat. Carl saw them and said, "Oh, that's Charlie."

Jim and Charlie got out and walked over to the group. In a gruff voice, Charlie said, "Hell no, you ain't sleepin' in my barn! After what Jim told me you did, going through all of the trouble to bring his brother back to him and his family, there is no way I would let you sleep out here. You all are going to spend the night up at the house with me and the Misses. She's gonna whip up a feast to send you all off right. After what you went through for the Rutherford's, you are all friends for life, as far as I am concerned."

Jim just stood there with a big smile on his face and said, "Now come on; everybody hop in the truck. We can come back down after dinner to shut the generator off. There should be a good charge on the battery by then."

With that, they all climbed in. Charlie took the front passenger seat, the ladies took the back seat, and Clint, Evan, and Jason jumped up into the pickup's bed. After the quick drive to the farmhouse, Jason took one look and said, "Now that is my idea of a dream home."

"Yeah, it's straight out of an old movie," said Carl.

The home was an old style, two-story farmhouse with a porch that wrapped all the way around. It had a chimney on each side of the house, as it had four fireplaces total for wood heat. Two fireplaces were located on each floor, one on each end of the house. As they went into the house, they felt as if they had stepped back in time. Oil lamps were in each room, giving them ample light and there was no television or other modern devices around that anyone could see at a glance.

Charlie had an old Civil War Springfield musket hanging over the main parlor's fireplace mantel. Jason walked up to it and said, "That looks like a real one."

"It is," said Charlie. "It has been in the family since the war. It's been handed down generation after generation. The Misses and I never had kids, though, so I'm the last of the line. I told her just to bury it with me," he said with a smirk on his face. "Besides, I might need it if the rapture doesn't go so smoothly."

They all shared a laugh, and then he led them into the kitchen. Charlie's wife, who he always just referred to as "the Misses," looked as if she was right out of history as well, standing there in a homemade dress, cooking over a real antique wood stove.

"Wow," Judith said. "This kitchen is amazing."

"Oh, thank you," said Charlie's wife. "I'm Clara; pleased to meet you."

As Judith ran her fingers across the intricate details of Clara's stove, she said, "Your home is just amazing, and this stove is unbelievable."

Clara smiled and said, "The stove was actually put in this house when it was built back in the mid-1800s. It's an antique just like me. I think you would probably have to tear a wall down just to get it out. And since we heat the house with wood anyway, we might as well throw a few logs on the stove every once in a while. It helps keep the kitchen warm, plus it's always ready to use that way."

"You seem well prepared for this type of situation, Charlie," Evan said.

"Well, it's easy to be old school when you never went new school in the first place," Charlie said. "We barely notice. We do have to keep an eye out for thieves and looters though. For some reason, some city people think they can just come take what we have once their precious supermarkets are emptied. It's like they think farmers are here to serve them or something. This is my damn farm, and I'll die protecting it if I have to!"

"Now, you old coot, just calm down," Clara said with her hands on her hips, giving him the eye.

Judith and Peggy helped Clara with dinner, which consisted of fresh steaks from a cow that they had just butchered, fresh-baked homemade bread, potatoes, carrots, and a homemade apple pie for desert. This was truly a feast for the group, as they had been living on tuna, oatmeal, and the like, pretty much since everything had gone down. While the men sat in the living room by the fire, Jim jokingly asked Charlie to come along with them on their boats.

He said, "Charlie, you and Clara need to come along with us. You're way too close to Wilmington and Philadelphia here to not have some sort of problems from people as they desperately leave the city in droves, looking for food. They will be like zombie hordes."

"Hell no, I ain't leavin'!" he said with a passion. "I've not got a whole lot longer on God's green earth as it is, and I'll be damned if I spend that time running. This farm is where I was born, and I can't think of a better place to die than right here on my family's land, defending it." All of the men just nodded in agreement and raised their coffee cups in a silent toast to honor what Charlie said.

After dinner, Clara showed the ladies to their quarters for the night while Jim took Evan and Jason back down to the barn to check on the battery and shut the generator off. As they got out Jim's truck, the noisy generator shut off on its own. They looked at each other and crept over to the barn. They saw three figures inside the barn. Evidently, the noisy generator had masked the sound of Jim's approaching F250 and the looters had not been alerted to their presence. Evan and Jason had foolishly left their rifles in the back of the Maule, but luckily, still had their Sigs holstered and ready to go.

As one of the men began to reach into the back of the Maule, Jason fired a shot at his feet and began to scream, "Down! Down! Down! Down on the floor or die where you stand!"

One of the other men immediately ran for the door. Jim grabbed a shovel that was hanging on the wall by the door and ran at the man, swinging it at him violently. He hit him in the head, making a loud metallic thump, instantly knocking the man unconscious as he plopped onto the floor of the barn, face down like a rag doll. He began hitting him in the back with the shovel over and over while screaming expletives in a fit of rage.

He then ran to the third man, who had dropped to his knees with his arms in the air in fear that Jason and Evan, who had now both drawn on them, would shoot. Jim rammed the shovel into his gut and kicked him in the face, knocking him backward onto the floor.

He approached the man by the Maule, who was now lying, face

down, with his hands spread. Jim grabbed him by the back of the head and started smashing his face into the dirt over and over, saying, "I swear to God almighty, if you or any of your looting scumbag friends ever come back here again, I will chop your arms and legs off, grind them up in a meat grinder, and force-feed them to you. I will kill you in the most horribly slow and disgusting manner that my war-torn, twisted mind can come up with. Do you understand me?"

The man couldn't answer because of the pummeling. Evan and Jason looked at each other in shock from seeing Jim snap like that, but they understood what Charlie and Clara meant to him, so they were not about to judge his defensiveness. He then took a five gallon jug of motor oil and poured it all over the three men while they lay there on the ground, cowering in pain. After he had exhausted the oil, he poured a can of paint thinner on them, then stood back and lit a cigarette.

At this point, Evan and Jason were about to intervene, when Jim said, "Now you two pick up your buddy there and drag his worthless ass off of this property as fast as you can. If you're not moving fast enough, I will light your asses on fire and laugh while I watch you burn to death. And you make sure you tell all of your scumbag friends they will not get the nice treatment you got. It will be much worse the next time I catch someone here." The two oil-covered men got up and struggled over to their unconscious accomplice, each grabbing an arm and began dragging him away. Jim followed them for a while, puffing on the lit cigarette to keep the fear of being burned alive fresh and real in their minds. After he was confident they wouldn't be stopping or turning around, he stopped following them but occasionally fired a shot at the ground just behind them to keep them motivated and moving.

He then walked back up to the barn with a look of disgust on his face and said, "Charlie wouldn't have been as polite and neighborly as I was."

"Damn, Jim," Jason said, "I sure would hate to be on your bad side."

"I take my loved ones seriously," he replied as he put the cigarette out on the wall.

Just then, Charlie and Carl came roaring up on one of Charlie's tractors. They slammed it to a stop and jumped off; Charlie, with his old side-by-side double barrel twelve-gauge shotgun, and Carl with his AK-74S. "What the hell were the shots for?" Charlie asked.

"There were a couple of thieves in the barn," Jim replied. "I guess they heard the generator running from a distance and decided to come and take it and see what else they could get."

Jason said, "Jim gave them a pretty good beat down and put the fear of God in them though, so I doubt they will be back."

"They may not be, but others from the cities will eventually," Jim replied.

"I'll just make a game out of them then," Charlie said. "It will help me pass the time. We old guys have to keep busy or we get bored."

"Well, let's get everything secured here and get you guys to bed. You have an eventful day ahead of you tomorrow," Jim said.

Having learned their lesson not to leave their gear unattended, Evan and Jason loaded all of their stuff back into Jim's truck to take back to the house with them for the night. They locked the barn back up with the chain on the door and drove up to the farmhouse.

Once the men came back into the house, the ladies asked them what all the commotion was about and Charlie said, "Oh, Jim just saw a coyote. He hates those things."

Judith and Peggy were relieved to think it was nothing, but Clara looked at Charlie with the stink eye, as she knew he wasn't being honest. He returned the look, and she understood. "Well, let's all get some sleep then," she said as they retired for the night.

Early the next morning, they were awakened by the smell of a freshly cooked breakfast coming from Clara's kitchen. She had made fried eggs that were freshly laid by their chickens, homemade biscuits, and steak medallions from the same cow they had enjoyed for dinner the previous night. Once everyone was up and about, she gathered everyone in the dining room and asked them to stand for a special prayer before the meal. Everyone joined hands and bowed their heads as Charlie said a profound prayer that brought tears to many of their eyes.

He said, "Dear Lord, our Father in Heaven, thank you for the abundance of this meal that we are about to eat. Thank you for granting us the fortune of growing up in a time and a place where we could learn the skills and the work ethic that it takes to provide for one's self and one's family in such abundance, while so many are scared and hungry and without the means or the knowledge to provide for themselves. Lord, please have mercy on those who have become dependent on society for their sustenance in this modern age, who have recently found themselves without a hand to feed them. Please help them and guide them in what you need them to do, in order to carry on in these uncertain and difficult times.

"Also, Lord, please help our new-found friends who have faced many difficult challenges, and who have found themselves joined together in this journey. Lord, we know the twists of fate that put them together had to be guided by your hand, and the events that brought them to Damon, and for Damon to help guide them to us. We know that their journey is part of a greater plan of yours, so please be with them and keep them safe. We thank you again, Lord, for our blessings and our friendships and family. In your name we pray, Amen."

Everyone in the room felt connected and somehow drawn together. When this whole chain of horrific events began, Evan, Jason, and Peggy were merely co-workers spending another day on the job together. Along the way, their lives had become intertwined with the Rutherford family, Judith, and now Charlie and Clara. Evan stood there in awe and reflected on their great fortune. To have somehow managed to be surrounded and helped by so many wonderful people throughout their perilous journey home staggered him. Humanity wasn't lost, not yet.

"Okay, everyone, let's eat," said Clara with a smile. And with that, they all sat down and enjoyed their wonderful breakfast and their beloved company.

After breakfast, Evan said, "Thank you all so much for the hospitality, but we had better get going. We've got a long way to go to get to Zanesville, and then on to Cincinnati and Tennessee."

They said their goodbyes to Charlie and Clara, and all loaded up in Jim's truck for the drive over to the barn. Once at the barn, Jim fired up the old Ford tractor and pulled it out of the way. They loaded their stuff into the back of the plane and then they all helped to push it out of the barn.

Peggy and Judith gave Jim and Carl a big hug. Judith said, "I'll say a little prayer each day that the *Little Angel* keeps you and your family safe."

Evan and Jason shook Jim's and Carl's hand and thanked them for everything. "Maybe we will see you guys again someday. Here is a map of where we will be. If the islands don't work out, feel free to come looking for us. You'll always have a place to go in Tennessee," said Evan as he handed them the map.

With that, they climbed into the Maule for the next phase of their journey. Excitement and anxiety overwhelmed them as they prepared to, yet again, venture off into the unknown.

Chapter 15: By the Air

"Well, here goes," said Evan. "Do you have the VFR sectional chart out so we can navigate via physical landmarks and terrain? That's all we will have to go on since all of the ground-based navaids, like VORs, are down without the electrical grid."

"Yep, I highlighted the route I think we should take. I'll keep my eyes on the ground and on the map, you just try to not hit anything staying low," Jason replied.

"What's a VOR?" asked Peggy from the back seat.

Evan turned around and said, "Oh, that stands for 'Very High-Frequency Omni-Directional Ranging.' It's a ground-based radio transmitter, the size of a small house that transmits a radio beam for each of the degrees on a compass rose. Combined with DME, or Distance Measuring Equipment, which most VORs have collocated with them, you can ascertain your exact position by determining the radial, or radio beam, you're on and the distance from the transmitter from the DME. Without DME, you can use intersecting radials from two different VOR transmitters, but it's just easier with DME. Our national airspace system of airways and intersections is basically made up by connecting the dots, going from one VOR transmitter to the next, tracking their radials as airways. GPS has been taking over, but the problem with that is with a flip of a government switch, the entire world's GPS satellite network goes down. With VORs, theoretically they can be run individually from the ground if need be. Hopefully, they get that sort of thing straightened out soon."

With Peggy being satisfied by his answer, Evan got back to the business of getting the Maule up and running. He pumped the carburetor primer three good times, then turned the start switch. The prop swooped around three times with no hits from the ignition. Evan gave the primer another two shots and turned the key again. On the second swing of the prop, the old Maule shook itself to life. After a moment of shuddering and shaking, it smoothed out and eventually purred like a big kitten. As soon as all of the operating temperatures and pressures were in range, Evan released the brake and taxied the plane across the grass field toward the strip. The strip hadn't been mowed or maintained for a while, but since it was late fall, the grass hadn't had much more growth since the last time it was cut. They could feel the resistance from the taller-than-normal grass during the taxi, but the Maule had ample power to overcome it.

"I hope that grass doesn't keep us on the ground too long, being heavy and all," Jason said.

Evan concurred and put in a notch of flaps to give them a little more slow speed lift. As he entered the runway strip, he took the turn under power and had the engine at full throttle by the time he lined up on the centerline and the Maule immediately began the roll. He held the yoke full forward, trying to get the tail off of the ground as soon as possible to reduce the drag from the grass to only the front two main wheels. In only a few hundred feet, the tail came off of the ground, leaving only the main wheels in the grass. He held the yoke with a little forward pressure to keep the plane glued and tracking straight while they continued to accelerate. At about three-quarters of the way down the grass runway, he felt like the plane was ready to fly. He snapped the nose off the ground, pitched up for a max performance climb, and quickly cleared the surrounding trees with ease. As soon as they got over the tree line safely, he leveled off and rocked the wings as a final wave goodbye to their friends down below.

He pulled the power back for a more efficient cruise, looked at Jason, and said, "Lead the way, Jason."

"Roger Roger," Jason responded with a renewed vigor in his voice.

Jason oriented their position to where they were on the chart and gave Evan suggested headings to get them going on the right track. With no electronic or radio navigation, it would be simple dead reckoning and pilotage with a lot of looking out the window and cross-referencing landmarks. Jason suggested a route which followed power lines that ran roughly in the direction of Zanesville for a while. Powerline access roads generally have the trees cleared on both sides of the lines, providing a clear path for them to fly extremely low while avoiding the trees.

They soon realized that the tree line access roads had become lines of drift for terrain-conscious travelers who were trying to get some mileage in while avoiding the main roads. "That's pretty dang smart," said Jason. "It's like a dirt highway."

"Yeah, and you can ditch into the woods in a hurry, like those people," Evan said, pointing at a campsite of about ten people who were scurrying into the trees to hide from them as they flew overhead. "They probably think we are authorities of some sort, scouting for people not complying with the new government mandates."

"Yep, just be glad they aren't shooting at us... yet," Jason said with his familiar crooked smile.

Peggy from the back seat said, "Yet? Shooting at us yet?"

"Relax, I'm just kidding... sort of," he replied with the same crooked smile.

"Whoa," Evan said as he dodged an antenna tower to the left. "Gotta remember those things don't have blinking lights on them right now. Where were you on that one, Mr. Navigator?"

"Sorry, captain. I was busy harassing the flight attendants. By the way, where is my coffee?" Jason said with a laugh as he turned and looked to the back seat.

"Ha, ha, ha," replied Peggy sarcastically.

They each settled into their thoughts for the next hour or so. They could see that so much of the America they loved was clearly in distress. They saw burned buildings and homes that were still smoldering on occasion. Evan wondered if they were set ablaze, or if they were accidentally burned down by people trying to use alternative methods of heating. It had been getting pretty cold at night, being this late in the year. There were cars abandoned virtually everywhere. Several gas stations had cars abandoned all around them. It was like people made it that far, desperately in search gas, only to find that there was none to be had. They saw a burned and destroyed police car with several bodies on the ground around it. They couldn't tell whether they were civilians or police officers, but considering the car was still there and burned, they figured it didn't end well for the police. At their low altitude, though, their view of things was limited as they would be passing over a scene by the time they even saw it.

"Okay, I think that is Lake Redman," Jason said, pointing out the window. "If that is the case, we are directly south of York, PA. That's about as far north as we want to go. If you stay on this heading, or maybe come about ten degrees left, we should hit the Pine Grove Furnace State Park soon. That will be an easy to recognize geographical feature. Then we will go from there, but I think we are doing good this way. Not far after that, we will be over the mountains of West Virginia, and then it is an easy hop over the mountains to Zanesville."

"Speaking of Zanesville," Evan said, "I think if we land this thing at the airport, we are putting ourselves at risk of arrest. We are heavily armed, with stolen government AR-15s I might add, and are flying against the presidential orders from the state of emergency. Considering that airports are the perfect secured staging ground for forward operating bases or any sort of government support activities, we should probably avoid them."

"Good point," said Jason. "Well, where do you want to put this thing down?"

"I think we need to consider this airplane as an asset that we don't want to give away as soon as we get out of it, and if we land at an airport or randomly on someone's property—that is basically what we will be doing. Does Ed still have that property east of Columbus?" Evan asked.

"Ed Savio?" Jason replied. "Yes, I believe he does."

"Could you identify it from the air?" Evan asked.

"Oh, hell yeah. I used to shoot there all the time with him. He has a range set up on his property and built a berm with a small bulldozer he rented. I'll be able to pick it out easy."

"Good, let's make that plan A unless we think of something else between here and there."

"Roger Roger," Jason replied sharply.

It didn't seem like much time passed before they identified the Pine Grove Furnace Park. Jason consulted the charts and they adjusted their heading accordingly to head generally toward Wheeling, West Virginia. They found that hugging the terrain over the mountains of West Virginia proved to be a little more challenging than they thought. Ducking below the hills sometimes meant a max performance climb in the overloaded Maule to get over the next rise or peak, giving Peggy and Judith a few scares they could have gladly done without. The airflow over the mountains that close to the terrain created quite a bit of uncomfortable turbulence for them as well. At one point, Judith had to be the first to utilize a sick sack. The sight and smell of it caused Peggy to do the same. The ladies weren't looking very well at all due to the rough ride.

Once they identified the Wheeling area, they were in the homestretch. Jason looked on the chart as to where he thought Ed's place would be. Using the Muskingum River as a reference, he pointed out the window and said, "I've got it! I know where his place is now. As soon as we get to the Muskingum River, turn north and we can parallel it to Ed's place," he said.

As they neared Zanesville, Jason's heart was racing with excitement. He was almost home. He hoped things were still okay there. "Okay, turn north now. You see that road off to your left?"

"Yep," Evan replied.

"Parallel that. The road will lead us to his place; I just don't think we should fly right up the middle of the road. Okay, now turn about thirty degrees to the left. Okay, go ahead and dirty up. We don't want to buzz around that place and draw attention. We need to drop right in over the tree line and put it down and shut it down on the spot the first time."

"Roger that," said Evan as he pulled the power back and began to slow to flap configuration speed. He fed in each notch of flaps on speed, then slowed for the next.

"Okay, that's the tree line there. Right on the other side of that is his property. His shooting berm is to the left, so try and hug the right side up against what looks like a fence line to the right. You're gonna have to dangle your wheels in those trees to get down quick enough."

"Are there any obstacles other than the berm I should know about?" asked Evan.

"Not that I can remember," Jason replied.

Evan slowed to about sixty knots and now had full flaps deployed. He pulled out the carburetor heat knob, double-checked everything, and said, "Okay, first landing in this thing and it's in someone's back yard at somewhere I've never been. Perfect."

Jason grinned as Evan lowered the airplane right to the tree line and said, "Dang, that's close."

Just as they passed the tree line, Evan chopped the power, kicked the rudder and put in opposite aileron to get the airplane into a forward slip, and dove for the ground. At just about the point of touchdown, he took the slip out, flared, and the aircraft firmly planted itself on all three wheels, then bounced once, and came back down to contact the ground right where some sort of hole had been dug. The right main gear dropped into the hole and bounced back out sending the airplane spinning around sideways. They slid across the wet morning grass, sideways, for about thirty feet. Finally, the opposite rudder input that Evan was holding brought the tail back around. The momentum swung the tail back around the other way as they slid to a stop, nearly ninety degrees sideways.

"And ladies and gentleman, we know you have a choice in air travel, and we hope you choose U.S. Scareways again for your next apocalyptic travel needs," Evan said in his best captain voice as Peggy swatted him in the back of the head.

Still laughing, Evan and Jason popped the doors open and began to climb out as a camouflaged ATV came roaring around the corner with a rifle laid across the handlebars. Evan and Jason could tell it was Ed frantically trying to see who had just performed an airborne invasion of his property.

As Ed slid to a stop, he said, "Oh my God! What in the world are you guys doing? Where the heck did you get a plane, and where did you come from? And why here?"

"Relax, man, we'll explain," Jason said, trying to calm him down. "Let's just get the ladies and our stuff out and hide this bird first."

"Of course," replied Ed quickly, formulating a plan.

Ed used his ATV to tow the Maule backward by tying a rope to the tail wheel and dragging the airplane through the wet grass. They pushed it into his hay barn and closed the doors to hide the plane from view. Ed then threw their bags on the racks of his ATV and drove their stuff to his house while they all followed behind on foot. Once they got inside, they caught him up on everything that had happened and how their amazing journey by land, by sea, and by air had gotten them this far. They asked him what he knew, and being sort of a connected fellow, he caught them up on things the best he could.

He said, "Well, in addition to what you already seem to know, there are a lot of reports that someone from the inside, here in the U.S., was providing the attackers—terrorists—or whatever you want to call them, with the weapons, logistics, and the support they needed to carry out such a simultaneous, widespread attack. All of it right under the noses of the federal government, without being detected. A few high-ranking officials who called things into question were shortly thereafter charged with crimes themselves and arrested. Some of the Border States that reported activity related to the border have had swarms of federal agents on the scene.

"Unfortunately, they didn't arrive to help the states secure the border, rather it is more what appears to be a takeover of those state governments. Though not directly, but indirectly, by arresting officials and even one governor for sedition and treasonous activities. Whether the charges are true or not, is irrelevant as due process seems to have been thrown out the window as well. A few of the governors in states like Tennessee, Georgia, and Texas have called up their national guards to defend the state capitols. They are refusing to let any federal agencies intervene, or even be on the Capitol grounds, after what has already happened in the other states. There is a total and utter breakdown of trust throughout all levels of the government.

"The only ones who act like they have total confidence in what is going on is the president's administration that continues, over and over again, to blame so-called homegrown insurgencies related to tea party groups. Many of the constitutional conservative organization leaders and various tea party group leaders have subsequently been arrested or are in hiding, fearing the same. What's even worse is that there are some reports of collusion between certain elements of the government and criminal elements."

"What do you mean?" asked Evan.

"Well, you know how the government had been on a campaign to track individuals and groups that stockpiled supplies, food, ammo, etc., and listed them as potential threats?"

"Yeah, that's why a lot of people refused to use credit cards and mail order for supplies," replied Jason.

"Right, well, from what I've heard through our state police here in Ohio, there have been elements of the government that may have unofficially shared their data on preppers and militia types with criminal enterprises, in order to encourage them to basically act as the privateers did during the Revolution and attack, harass, rob, etc., people with stockpiles of supplies."

"Why the heck would our own government do that? That just doesn't make any sense," said Peggy.

"Well, think about it. This is the same government that shipped assault weapons to Mexican drug cartels and gave weapons to known Al-Qaeda affiliates by calling them freedom fighters in Syria and Libya. They have been hell-bent on getting the American people as dependent on the government as they can, which, of course, translates into control. So the reason they have been on a negative propaganda campaign against survivalists and preppers, is that those folks will be the hardest—and last—ones they are able to gain control over.

"They know that, chances are, they will never convince them to willingly follow their line of thinking, and if there were to be an armed insurgency against their ever-increasing iron grip on the American people, they're the people who will be leading the charge. In essence, they use criminals and other groups, not affiliated directly with the government, to do their bidding for them. All they have to do is share the information on where the food, weapons, and ammo stockpiles are and insinuate that they will look the other way. The next thing you know, those people become prime targets for hostile looting activities. It's not a new concept. The British and Colonial governments both used such tactics during the Revolution, and we even recently used the same sort of tactics against the Soviets during their war in Afghanistan. We gave weapons and intelligence to the Mujahedeen, and they did our dirty work for us, all while we could deny having involvement. The strategy really has been used countless times throughout history.

"This complete and utter meltdown and mistrust between the different branches of state, local, and federal government, has all available resources focused on the capitols and major metropolitan areas. The outlying and rural areas have pretty much become a dog-eat-dog version of the Wild West, with some towns setting up militia groups for defense. Some of these groups are led by sheriffs, and some by civilian groups, sealing off entry by outsiders until it all settles down. Some other towns have almost literally been burned to the ground by looters, rioters, and the like. It's not a pretty picture, and I really can't see how any of this is going to blow over anytime soon."

"I'm surprised the president hasn't gotten UN troops on the

ground as so called 'peacekeepers' yet," responded Jason.

"Oh, the blue helmets are coming, from what I have heard," Ed continued. "My position with the state has me privy to some of the information flowing from the governor's office. The governor, himself, isn't on good terms with this administration, so he has pretty much been sequestered away and is communicating with the Ohio State Police and Ohio National Guard remotely. That's how a lot of the information has gotten to me. It has to pass through a lot of hands, what with secure electronic communications being out of the picture."

"By the way, don't drink the water. There are reports of a lot of people getting sick and dying from the water in a few of the Columbus suburbs. I haven't heard anything about here, or where you live, Jason, but you don't want to be one of the first to find out the hard way that your water supply has been compromised."

"We've got to get on the road," Jason said. "I've got to get to my family."

Ed looked at his old friend, Jason and said, "Hey man, take that old Ford F100 pickup out back. It's a total jalopy and isn't tagged, but it's not like that matters. It should have enough gas to get down the road to your house."

"Thanks, man, you're a hell of a friend. Can we leave the plane here for now? We will eventually come back for it but not sure when at this point," asked Jason."

"Sure thing. Are you bug'n out once you get there?"

"Yep, we are heading toward Cincinnati to drop Peggy and Judith off and then heading down to Tennessee to Evan's place to ride everything out together," Jason replied. "You should come with us, or at least consider it as a bug out location, if you need it."

"I'll keep that in mind, Jason, thanks." He then scratched his chin and said, "Cincinnati, huh?" Ed questioned with a concerned look on his face.

"Yes, Cincinnati, why?" asked Peggy in a very serious manner.

"Well, from the info I got from the governor's office, there isn't much left of Cincy. There were some pretty massive explosions in the center of the city and the place was just about burned to the ground. Add to that the population of thugs and wannabe gang bangers there, and it's just not a pretty picture. There was quite a bit of rioting and looting. All of this has been going on for so long now that the thugs know they have free reign to do whatever they want. No law enforcement is coming for them. All of the law enforcement activity right now is all political; they aren't concerned with crime in the least. Anyway, most of the city from what I know, has been abandoned and the casualty rate is quite high."

The group just stood there with a look of horror on their faces, digesting all of the information Ed shared with them. They had been in the dark about a lot of things this whole time, and this was a lot to take in.

"The Kentucky National Guard was immediately posted on the Kentucky side of the river to keep the mayhem from crossing over the bridges," Ed continued. "I guess the river was a pretty good natural barrier, keeping most of the violence on the Ohio side."

"Oh, thank God," said Peggy. "My parents have my son and they live on the Kentucky side, in Newport."

"Well, I don't know much about the Kentucky end of things," he said. "My sources are only versed in Ohio state matters, so hopefully your family is okay."

Jason said, "Thanks, Ed. Do you want us to bring your truck back here?"

"No, man, you don't need to waste time with that. Just leave it at your place and I'll know where to find it if I really need it," he said.

"You guys grab your gear and head on over to the truck and load up. I'll go grab the keys," Ed said as he turned and walked to the house.

Evan, Jason, Judith, and Peggy each grabbed their packs and walked to the truck. They threw everything in the back as Evan said, "Jason, you drive since you're the only one with a clue as to where we are going. Peggy and Judith, you ride up front in the cab with Jason, and I'll be the trunk monkey, or rather the bed monkey, in the back providing cover."

"Good idea," replied Jason. "And let's keep our weapons out of sight, but at the ready. No need to ruffle feathers around here if we don't need to. Most people around here are good people."

Just then, Ed came walking up with the keys and tossed them to Jason. He shook Evan's and Jason's hands, gave both of the ladies a quick hug, and said, "You two ladies take care of these guys. They are a little off their rockers and need to be babysat."

Peggy and Judith laughed and said, "Oh yeah, we've noticed that more and more every day."

Jason fired up the old Ford and headed out of Ed's driveway. Everyone gave Ed a wave goodbye as he watched them drive away. "Crazy bastards," he said under his breath as he turned and walked back into the house.

Chapter 16: The Reunion

Jason pulled out of Ed's driveway and, after taking a few turns on some backroads, they came out on North River Road, which would take them south most of the way toward his house. Evan pecked on the back window and Jason reached back and slid it open.

Evan said, "Ohio 666! Really? That's the road we are taking?" That was the official road name of North River Road, according to the street sign. Jason just laughed and gave him a crooked smile, then went back to driving.

They paralleled the river via North River Road for several miles. It was mostly uneventful, with the occasional abandoned car left on the shoulder. They assumed it was someone who ran out of gas before they could get to where they were going. "Okay, there is Jaycee Riverside Park," Jason said with anxiety. "We are almost there." He took a left and then an immediate right onto Zane Street, and then took another left onto a smaller road that would lead them to his neighborhood while avoiding the more congested areas.

He rounded the corner only to have to slam on the brakes because a pickup truck was sitting sideways in the middle of the road, along with a few large fellows with shotguns and hunting rifles. "This road is closed," one of them shouted.

"It's not closed to me. I live this way," replied Jason with authority.

"Turn around," the man ordered again as he repositioned his shotgun.

Evan eased up out of the bed of the truck and rested his AR-15 on the top of the cab, not pointing it at the men, but letting them know the discussion was not going as they had planned. Jason opened the truck door, got out and walked right up to the man, pulling out his wallet as he approached. The men tightened their grips on their guns as if they were preparing to be attacked. The apparent leader of the group seemed to pay extra attention once he noticed Jason's Sig holstered on his side.

Jason pulled his driver's license out of his wallet and put it up to the face of the man giving the orders and said, "Look! See my address? I live just a mile or so down the damn road, so move out of the way! I have come a long damn way to get back to my wife and kids and I'll be damned if you are gonna be another obstacle in my way."

The man looked at his driver's license, turned to the other men, and motioned to move aside. They pulled the truck that was blocking the road back just enough to let the F-100 through. Jason got back in the truck and pulled up to the men. "I appreciate what you are doing," he said before he drove away.

As they entered the residential area, they could see that a few of the homes had been recently burned to the ground. I hope those were just accidents, Evan thought to himself. He couldn't dare imagine anything having happened to Jason's family. Jason was a time bomb waiting to explode as it was. Jason weaved around a few cars that were left abandoned in the road.

One man on the sidewalk yelled, "Sell me a gallon of gas!" but Jason just kept driving. As he pulled onto his street, his heart was beating faster than he had ever felt it. He pulled into the driveway and was relieved to see that his wife's car was still parked in front of the garage. The garage door was closed, so he assumed his truck was still inside. His airport car had been left in employee parking in Columbus, and he planned on just leaving it there. It wasn't worth risking anyone's life to go into the city to get it.

He jumped out of the cab of the truck and went over to the side gate that led into the backyard. He expected to see his dog, Browning. He would usually be standing on his hind legs, leaning on the fence, excited to see him, but it was eerily quiet. This made him a little concerned. He put his hand on his pistol and walked over to the kitchen door on the side of the house and noticed damage around the edge of the door by the bolt.

He yanked the door open and ran inside, with Evan following

with his AR at the ready. Jason drew his pistol and yelled, "Shit!" He pointed it at a body on the floor, then quickly scanned the rest of the room. The man was lying in a pool of blood and appeared to be dead. He ran toward the bedroom screaming, "Sarah! Sarah! Sarah!" He ran into the bedroom to find his wife and two sons cowering in the corner, crying.

As soon as they recognized him, his boys jumped up and ran to him screaming, "Daddy! Daddy! Daddy!" and jumped into his arms.

His wife was getting up to join them, and he noticed blood all over her. He dropped his sons to their feet and ran over to help her. "I'm okay, I'm okay," she said, giving him a huge hug and began to cry tears of joy.

"Are you hurt?" he asked frantically.

"No... no, it's his blood."

"Whose blood? The man in there?" Jason said as he pointed toward the living room.

"Yes, it was Brandon Murphy from down the street, he broke in last night," she said as he wiped the tears from her cheek. They just held each other for a moment while Evan swept the rest of the house to make sure it was secure. He then came into the bedroom to let Jason know it was all clear.

Sarah began to explain to them what had happened. She told him all about Brandon's odd behavior a few days before, how she had found Browning sick, and that the rabbits were missing. She told him that later that night, Browning passed away. She then went on to say, "Last night at about 2 am, Kevin said he was thirsty so I got up to get him a glass of water from the kitchen. That's where I found Brandon and another man loading food into a bag. I screamed out of reflex and Brandon grabbed me and tried to cover my mouth. He was squeezing me so tight, I could barely breathe so I bit his hand. He pulled out a knife and put it to my throat and told me to shut the hell up or he would gut me like a pig in front of the boys.

"Just then, I saw a flash of light and heard a loud pop. Brandon went limp and fell to the floor, and there stood Michael with your

.45. He looked scared to death. He had just shot Brandon in the side, right through the ribs at point-blank range. The other man must have run because I turned around and the door was open and he was gone. I didn't know for sure, though, so I grabbed Michael and ran back into the bedroom. We've been hiding in here with your gun ever since. I'm so glad you're home. Oh, I knew you would come back to us." She broke down crying and collapsed into his arms.

Evan excused himself to give them some space and said, "I'll give you a moment. I'll go check on Peggy and Judith." He went back out front where Peggy and Judith were still sitting in the truck. He went over and sat down in the driver seat and explained everything to them.

"Oh my God," Peggy said.

"I'm so glad they are okay," said Judith. "I can't imagine what Jason would have done without them."

"Neither can I," Evan replied.

After a few moments, the front door of the house swung open and out came Jason, dragging Brandon's body by the arms. He pulled him out into the street, turned, and walked back into the house like he was on a mission. As Evan sat there wondering if he should go in and see if there was anything he could do, Jason came back out the front door with a piece of wooden furring strip and a small piece of plywood. He broke the furring strip over his knee making a sharp, jagged edge on the end of the stick. He then laid it on the street, nailed the plywood to it, and then placed it over Brandon's back. He drove it through Brandon's body with a few solid hits of the hammer. He then stood up and deliberately walked back into the house without saying a word. Evan had gotten out of the truck when Jason had come back outside the first time. He walked over and looked at the plywood. It had a message written on it with a marker that said, "This is what happens when you touch my family."

Evan walked back over to the door that Jason had left open and knocked on the door frame. Jason said, "Come on in. Sorry about that; I just had to deal with a few things."

"No problem, man, I understand," Evan replied.

Sarah came out of the bedroom. She had changed clothes and cleaned herself up. Jason introduced Peggy and Judith to Sarah, and they all caught Sarah up on what had happened during their trip. While the ladies got to know each other, Evan and Jason cleaned up the mess in the kitchen that was left by the previous night's altercation. They also fixed the kitchen door frame and re-locked all of the doors.

Jason fired up his generator that he had wired into the house via a twist lock plug that hooked to a manual switch-over box. "Give it about a half hour, and there should be plenty of hot water for people to start taking showers. Just don't swallow any of the tap water, just in case. Evan, let's walk out to the shed," said Jason.

He and Evan walked out back, unlocked the shed, and went inside. This was where Jason had his HAM radio setup. "Try and get in touch with Molly if you want, but it's past 9 am, so I doubt they are on there, but you never know. I think we should get on the road soon. I know Sarah and the kids aren't comfortable here now. After everyone is washed up and we eat dinner, I think we need to load up and go. We can take the Dodge and you can follow along in Sarah's car, now that we have extra bodies to haul. Having to make a stop in Newport, Kentucky, is going to throw our bug out route all out of whack, but it is what it is," Jason said.

Evan got on the HAM radio and tried to reach Molly to no avail. He didn't really expect to, though, as it wasn't their agreed upon monitoring time. She also had a lot to do around the Homefront, with all of the kids and animals. Hopefully, he would be there in a day or two at the most now, anyway.

Everyone took turns taking a nice, hot shower. It was a refreshing change from the recent norm. Judith gathered up everyone's dirty clothes and washed them, using Sarah's washer and dryer, thanks to the generator. The dryer really bogged down the generator from its wattage use, but they just did not have the time to wait for all of the clothes to line dry.

Peggy was the last to get out of the shower. Once she got all cleaned up and dressed, she came out of the bathroom and said with a smile, "You really don't realize how bad you must have smelled until you get a shower and fresh, clean clothes. So, how long do you think it will take us to get to Newport?" Peggy was clearly anxious to get home to her son and parents, who she had been completely out of contact with during this entire ordeal.

"Well, back before the world fell apart, it would have only taken two and a half hours at highway speed via the interstate. There is no chance we can risk going through Columbus and Cincinnati, though, with things the way they are there. Not to mention all of the obstacles we can expect to find along the way; it could take a day or more. To get around those two cities, we are going to need to go well out of our way to the south and then over to the west," replied Jason, trying not to paint too negative of a picture.

"Peggy, how do you and Judith feel about carrying a gun now?" Evan asked.

"I've never shot a gun before," she sheepishly replied.

"Well, considering the state of things, and the fact that we will now be traveling in two vehicles, with Jason in one and me in the other, I think we need to get everyone armed for the trip," he said.

"My husband and I used to go to the range and shoot his handgun sometimes," replied Judith. "I'd feel better if I had one."

"Okay then, while Jason and his family are packing their stuff up and getting ready to hit the road, let's go out back and go over a few things." With that, Evan took the ladies into the backyard and introduced them to a few of Jason's extra guns. He gave them a quick, down-and-dirty lesson on the operation of the SKS rifle. He had them practice loading with stripper clips and also with the detachable thirty-round magazines that Jason had for them. Jason normally kept the ten-round built-in magazine on them, however, being in their originally imported configuration, they didn't meet compliance with section 922r. Regulatory compliance seemed to be a moot point at the moment, however, so in his mind, 922r was not an issue.

In addition to the SKSs, Evan taught them the operation of the M1911 pistol. Jason's personal handgun was a Springfield Armory TRP 1911, but he also had picked up three Rock Island Armory GI style 1911s over the past few years. They weren't the pride and joy of his collection, but he figured if it ever got to the point where he needed them, he wouldn't be concerned about the fit and finish of the Philippine made guns. They were reliable and solid performers and were acquired at a budget price that allowed him to purchase three of them. This made them more valuable to the mission at hand than one high-end gun. Evan had them practice with snap caps, dry firing, and clearing simulated malfunctions until they felt reasonably comfortable with them.

When the ladies were positive they were ready to handle them, he gave them each a pistol in an old government surplus holster and two double magazine pouches each, which were also surplus items. This gave them each a total of four magazines, loaded with 230 grain .45ACP ball ammo. "From here on out, these things don't leave your side," he said to them with a serious look. "We've got a long way to go, and as we get closer to Newport, things will only get more dangerous." The two ladies looked at each other with a sense that the intensity of their journey wouldn't be letting up anytime soon, and having the need to carry their own gun just drove that point home even further.

They went back into the house to find that the Jones family had been pre-packed so well that they were pretty much ready to go. Jason said, "The Dodge's regular fuel tank and the auxiliary tank are both full, they stay that way. I have enough gasoline in the shed that I had around for the generator to top off Sarah's car. We can also put a few gas cans in the rooftop carrier as well as one or two in the back of the truck. That should be enough to get both vehicles all the way to Tennessee. Evan, if you want to drive Sarah's car you can put all of your bags in the trunk, and I can keep all of our stuff in the back of the truck underneath the sleeping bed."

"All that work you put into that truck is about to pay off big time," said Evan.

"Yep, I wish I never needed it, but here we are, so I'm glad I did. Let's get a move on; this place just doesn't feel like home to me anymore. Let's eat dinner and get on the road."

With that being said, they all went inside. While the women were in the kitchen preparing dinner, Evan and Jason sat in the living room with the boys to go over an atlas to try and come up with the best route to Newport.

"It looks like zigging and zagging all over the place is really the only way to get there without taking the interstate. There isn't a direct path," said Evan while studying the Ohio section of the atlas.

"I know," replied Jason. "I was also thinking that we need to find a staging point to park the Dodge and leave Sarah and the kids while we run into Newport to drop off Peggy and Judith. I don't think it would be smart to drag everyone into there."

"I agree," Evan said. "Although I recommend we take that precaution one step further and leave you with them to protect them. They have been through enough already, and now that you have made it home to them, you need to be there for them. I can escort Peggy and Judith into Newport and get back out to meet up with you, and then we can continue south to Tennessee together."

"I can't let you go in there alone," Jason said.

"Well, that's just how it's gonna be. We will make a rendezvous time and if I'm not back by then, you fire up the Dodge and head on south without me, If something happens to me, I want you at the Homefront helping to keep my family safe," Evan said in a serious voice.

"Sounds reckless, yet prudent at the same time... so deal, I guess," Jason said reluctantly.

After dinner, they all loaded up their stuff and climbed into the vehicles. Jason walked over to Sarah's car and handed Evan a walkie-talkie. "The car has a CB radio mounted in it and so does the Dodge so we can communicate as a convoy. If, for some reason, we need to get off of the CB because we feel it's not secure, or if we get separated outside of our vehicles, use these." Evan nodded in agreement as Jason looked inside the car and said, "You ladies ready?"

"Roger Roger!" Peggy said, followed by a laugh.

"Are you mocking me?" asked Jason with a serious look on his face.

"Absolutely," she said.

"Okay then, as long as we got that straightened out," he said with his crooked smile as he turned and hopped in the Dodge. With a nod, he fired it up and pulled away. Evan put the car into drive and off they went in trail.

Chapter 17: By the Land

It took a little over an hour to get clear of Zanesville. It was slow going. They encountered a few of the neighborhood watch style road blocks like the one they had dealt with earlier, but none of them held them up for long. Just on the outskirts of Zanesville, at least ten government helicopters flew overhead at treetop level in a tight formation. "I bet they are heading for Columbus," Jason said over the CB.

"Were those state or federal?" asked Evan in response.

"Not sure, but if they are federal I can't see anything good coming of it, from what we have heard. Good thing we are moving on," replied Jason.

Once they were clear of Zanesville, the rural backroads were uneventful and they were making good time. They had been traveling almost two hours and were now in the hilly to mountainous terrain of southeastern Ohio, when they came around a blind corner and nearly hit an SUV that was rolled over on its top, straddling the road and blocking both lanes. Evan slammed on his brakes, narrowly avoiding rear ending Jason's truck. Evan instinctively threw the car into reverse and began retreating backward, and Jason did the same.

"What's wrong?" asked Judith. "Why aren't we stopping to see if anyone is hurt?"

"Didn't you see the bullet holes in the glass and the doors?" Evan replied. Just then, they heard gunshots off in the distance. Evan floored it and backed up as fast as he could until they went around a curve, where they had terrain for natural cover. He pulled off against the side of the hill, grabbed his rifle, and jumped out of the car, taking cover while assessing the situation.

Jason backed around the corner in the Dodge with smoke billowing out of the hood. His family exited the truck and climbed in the back while he walked around, flipping down his hinged armor panels that were attached to the cargo rack around the truck's canopy. He then jogged over to Evan, cussing under his breath. "I don't think we should just turn around. They could have buddies behind us waiting for us to return and we need to check my truck out. I would feel much safer fixing my truck in a secure environment rather than waiting to be shot in the back while my head is under the hood. I don't want to keep running scared all day either. I'm sick of this shit," Jason said in an agitated manner.

"What's your plan?" Evan asked.

"Peggy, you and Judith get in the back of the truck with Sarah and the boys. That steel will keep you safe. Evan, you climb up on the top of this hill and cover them from the high ground while providing me with suppressing fire if it comes to that. I'm gonna grab my Remy and try to get into a position where I can pick those guys up with my Nightforce scope. I have a general idea where they might be," said Jason as he jogged back over to his truck to get his Remington.

"Sounds like a plan," responded Evan.

Peggy and Judith climbed into the back of Jason's truck while Jason reached underneath the sleeping platform and pulled out his Remington 700. He also grabbed a bandoleer loaded with .300 Winchester Magnum rounds, gave Evan a pat on the shoulder, and took off into the woods. His plan was to double back for a bit and then head up to the high ground and follow the ridgeline on the opposite side from the shooters, hoping to get a view of them through his high-powered Nightforce scope.

It took him about twenty minutes, creeping along the ridge, using the natural lines of the terrain as cover. Once he got into position, he glassed the area where he thought the shots came from. He didn't see anything at first, but from his experience as a hunter, he knew just to be still, calm, and patient and your prey will eventually make a mistake and present itself.

After approximately ten minutes of nothing, he saw a glint of light just to the right of where he was looking. It came from behind a tree on top of a ridgeline on the opposite side of the road from his position. Figuring it was a reflection of the sun from a rifle optic or some binoculars, Jason focused on it and then zoomed his powerful Nightforce scope in a bit more. He wasn't afraid of making the same mistake as they had, giving their position away from a reflection. They had made the tactical error of setting up on a hill, that as they day progressed, put the sun out in front of them instead of at their backs. The sun was now at Jason's back, giving him the advantage. Also, his Nightforce scope had a flash killer attached to it, hiding light reflections with a honeycomb-patterned louver.

As he zoomed in and focused, he saw that it was, indeed, a rifle pointed toward the curve in the road where they were ambushed. Jason reached into his rifle scabbard and pulled out his suppressor. He threaded the sound suppressor on to the end of his rifle to try to help conceal his position as long as he could, thereby retaining the tactical advantage. He then took aim back on his target, timed his breath, and eased his trigger back until his rifle let loose its one hundred and eighty grain open tip boat tail projectile, screaming at his target at nearly three thousand feet per second, almost instantly hitting the assailant and knocking him back into the woods, out of sight. Jason immediately scanned the surrounding area, hoping the impact would flush out any other targets. He saw movement to the left, cycled another round, and let it fly. This time he could clearly see his target fall to the ground and roll down the hill. It was a man dressed in hunting style camouflage with an AR-15. Once the man came to a stop, Jason saw him try to crawl a few feet and then just stop. He put another round in the man's back just to make sure he wasn't playing dead.

He continued his intense surveillance of the area for another ten minutes and didn't see any more movement. Confident that he had neutralized the threat, he slipped back over the back side of the ridge, tossed the rifle in the scabbard, threw it on his back, and then jogged through the woods back to the truck. He put his Remington back in the truck and grabbed his AR-15. He signaled for Evan to join him and they both snuck down to the ambush site to make sure it was all clear.

Once they got within visual range, they took cover and scanned the area with binoculars. They couldn't see any movement, so while Jason covered Evan, he slipped over to the overturned SUV to make sure it was clear inside. To his horror, he saw that there was a family with a small child inside, all dead. Off to the side of the road were some pieces of luggage that looked like they had been thoroughly rummaged through for anything of value. This enraged Evan. All he could think about was how that family's future was stolen from them for a few basic items.

He ran back toward Jason and they took cover behind some rocks on the side of the road, just at the apex of the curve. "There is an entire family dead in that thing. Those bastards look like they just picked them off while they were driving, came down and pillaged their truck, then went back up on the hill to wait for the next victims to happen by, which unluckily for them, was us. Let's check out your truck and get moving."

"Roger Roger," responded Jason as they pulled back from their position to the truck. They popped the hood on his Dodge and saw that the smoke was an oil mist from a hole blasted in the valve cover of the big diesel six cylinder.

"Thankfully, they were using .5.56 ARs. By the time that little 55 grain bullet ripped through your hood and impacted the valve cover, there wasn't enough of anything left to keep going. The smoke must have just been oil mist blowing out of the hole and then cooking off on the hot turbo. Looks like one grazed the block over there, but other than that, we can patch this up and get going. Got any more of that speed tape?" Evan asked Jason.

"Sure do," Jason said as he jogged to the back of his truck, then returned with a shiny new roll of metal tape.

Evan cleaned off the valve cover the best he could with some Gun Scrubber that Jason also had brought along, which is basically just a very clean degreaser similar to brake cleaner. They wiped it dry and then put multiple layers of the speed tape over the hole, weaved in every direction. "That should do it," he said, handing the tape and cleaner back to Jason. They checked and topped off his engine oil, fired the truck up, checked the integrity of the tape, and got on the road again.

They crept around the overturned SUV in their vehicles off to the side of the road, dropping slightly off of the shoulder to get around. Once clear, Jason put the hammer down and with a dark cloud of diesel smoke billowing out of his exhaust, he pulled away with Evan in trail. The rest of the day fell into the darkness and was mostly uneventful. They passed some people walking on the side of the road at times, but no one showed them any aggression, just lots of desperate souls on the move.

At about midnight, they passed a man, a woman, and two small children walking on the side of the road, pulling wheeled suitcases along behind them. Jason slowed his truck and came to a stop, Evan slowing along behind him. The family was startled and ran off into the woods to avoid them. By this point, most people had learned that a mistrust of others was a healthy way to go about your day. Jason got out, walked to the back of his truck, reached in, and pulled out a bag containing some venison jerky, granola bars, and a few bottles of water. He set it down on the edge of the road and yelled off into the trees. "It's okay. No one here is going to hurt you. There is food and water in this bag for your kids. After we drive away, please come and get it."

He then walked back to his truck, got in, and they drove away. He looked into his rear-view mirror, hoping to catch a glimpse of them retrieving the food, but it was too dark. He just said a silent prayer that God would bring them back to the road, for them to find the food for their children. Jason couldn't imagine the hopeless feeling of being a parent in such a desperate situation.

At around 3 am they were nearing the town of Cherry Grove. The emptiness of the rural roads were long behind them as they began to get into more and more densely populated areas. Jason pulled off into a burned down gas station parking lot and Evan pulled up alongside. Evan got out and met Jason at the front of the truck. They pulled out the atlas and began to look it over.

"Well, we are almost there, and the way I see it, I'm going to have to get on I-275 at some point. Without getting further north toward Cincinnati, I'm gonna have to cross the river at the I-275 bridge crossing. If what Ed told us about the Kentucky National Guard having the border secured is correct, that could be a good thing. I'll show them my badge and play it off like I am a regular Federal Air Marshal and tell them I have to get to the airport where I've been ordered to report. Hopefully, that will work. Considering the fact that we can also expect a heavy Kentucky National Guard presence, I'm gonna leave my AR here and just take the SIG since it's backed up by my credentials," Evan said.

"How many rounds do you have left?" asked Jason.

"I've got nearly two full mags."

"Here," Jason said, handing Evan his remaining one-and-a-half mags of .40. "I've got a truck full of guns here, if that is all you are gonna have, then take as much as you can."

Evan took the magazines, placed them in his cargo pocket, and said, "Well, looking at where we are, there is a tract of sparsely inhabited land down on Eight Mile Road just on the south side of I-275 here." Evan pointed at the map. "You and your family find a place to lie low there and keep your CB on. Get a good night's sleep and if you don't see me by sundown tomorrow night, just head on down to Tennessee without me."

"Take care of Peggy and Judith," Jason said as he gave both of the women a hug. Peggy and Judith said their goodbyes to Sarah and the boys and then got in the car and drove away with Evan, off into the distance, not knowing if they would ever see the Jones family again.

Chapter 18: Not So Quiet On the Homefront

Down in Tennessee, Molly had been keeping busy with the kid's homeschool routine, as well as keeping up the animals. Griff had pretty much taken over all of the security duties and had been using Jake and Greg as sentries as well. He used Jake during the daytime, and he and Greg split the watch at night. They kept to the property, not venturing out. They had everything they needed and didn't want to take on any unnecessary risks. Molly was both worried and excited since making contact with her husband. She was happy to have heard from Evan back in Delaware, but had no idea how far he had gotten, or if things had gone well at all. She tuned in every morning to listen for word from Evan, but day after day, she heard nothing but static. After about an hour of waiting, her routine was to scan through other known channels to try to find out what was going on in the outside world. She had heard some pretty disturbing reports about what was going on out there but didn't quite know what to believe, so she just hoped for the best.

It was a beautiful morning, and she followed her regular routine out by the chicken coop, collecting eggs with Lilly. Sammy was inside with Griff's wife, Judy. Judy had been a huge help around the house since they had been there. Just as Lilly was reaching in to collect an egg for her mommy, Molly heard a gunshot that sounded like it came from the front of the house, followed by several rapid-fire shots, and then another. It sounded like two different guns to her, so she dropped the egg basket, grabbed Lilly, and ran for the house.

As she started to enter the back door, Griff came around the corner hoping on one leg with blood running down his pants. "What's going on?" she said as Lilly started crying from all of the commotion.

"Just get in!" he shouted as he pushed her into the house,

following along behind and holding his leg. Once inside, Griff yelled for Greg and Jake, who were already running in to meet him from hearing the gunshots. "Boys, go get downstairs," he said. They all ran downstairs, joined by Judy, who had Sammy, and took up a position in the basement where the communications and observation equipment was located. They locked all of the other doors behind them. Ever since the run-in with the van, they had been keeping the reinforced shutters closed and all of the exterior doors and deadbolts locked. This meant they could rest assured, knowing the state of material readiness of the rest of the house without having to go and check.

Molly powered on the perimeter trail cams and the close-in infrared cameras to assess the situation while Judy began to check Griff's wounds and administer first aid. "Looks like it went clean through your leg and missed your femur, thank goodness," Judy said. What happened?"

Griff applied pressure to the wound while they waited on Molly to take a look. "I was walking out to check the lock on the gate as usual, when I guess I surprised those guys as they came around the corner heading for the gate. One of them pulled a rifle up—an AK, I think—and popped off a couple shots, one got me as I turned to run," he explained.

She then ran and grabbed Molly's trauma kit and started getting him patched up for the moment, to at least get the bleeding to stop. "This will do for now. Let me know if you start feeling funny or anything," she said as she applied the dressing.

Molly scanned the cameras, looked at Griff, and said, "Can you walk? Can you get around?"

"Sure, what do you need?" he asked.

She tossed him a handheld radio and said, "There are several trucks at the gate. It looks like they are trying to cut the lock."

Griff said, "I'm on it. Jake, go get me your Dad's .50 cal and a VZ58 and plenty of ammo. Greg, you go with him and grab a VZ for each of you. Help him carry it all." In just a few moments, Greg and Jake came back into the basement with everything Griff had ordered. "Now, Jake, you stay here and guard the women and girls; you're the last line of defense. Greg, help me carry this stuff up to the top floor."

Greg and Griff took the fifty, their two VZ58 rifles, and several cans of ammo up to the top floor of the house where they would have the best vantage point. Griff took the fifty caliber rifle out of its case, loaded a single round into the chamber, and aimed the rifle through the shooting cross cut into the reinforced shutters. He aimed at the man cutting the lock and eased the trigger back until a thundering boom resulted in the man's left arm being torn clean off at the shoulder.

"A little left, Dad," Greg said.

"Yes, I see that. I'm a little unstable trying to hold this thing up with a bum leg. Go into one of the other rooms and grab me a table and some stuff that I can stack up to make a rest even with these shooting ports."

As Greg ran off to get what his dad needed, Griff looked through the shooting port with the scope of the rifle to see that the other men had scattered and the man who lost his arm was lying on the ground, writhing in pain. Greg came back into the room with a child's desk and some books to put under the bipod legs to prop it up to the proper height. Griff and Greg got the fifty all set up, then he took aim again at the man on the ground. With another thunderous boom, he blew his heart clean out of his chest, ending the suffering. Griff picked up the radio and called down to Molly. "Do you see anything?"

"No one else is at the front gate or near the house, but I can see a man out in the woods on one of the trail cams. We can't reach him from here because of the woods and terrain, but at least we can tell they haven't left."

Molly, being a nurse, then asked Judy to come over and keep an eye on the monitors while she went upstairs to check on Griff's wound. She took her trauma kit with her and cleaned up the wound the best she could under the circumstances and dressed it properly.

"We'll do better later, but this will keep you from falling apart for now," she said as she handed him some ibuprofen for the pain. "I would give you something stronger, but I need you to keep your head in the game."

"Oh, I'll be fine. Greg and I will sit up here and keep watch for a while if you want to go back and hunker down in the basement with the kids. If we need anything, we will let you know." Molly then rejoined the others in the basement while they waited to see what the intruder's next move would be.

Chapter 19: Newport

The Jones family followed the plan and drove down Eight Mile Road until they found a dirt side road that went about two hundred yards, before coming to a dead end. He turned the truck around, shut everything off, and said to Sarah, "You and the kids climb in the back and get some sleep. I'll stay up and stand watch. In the morning when the sun comes up, we can figure out how to get into a better position to keep an eye out for Evan to return."

She kissed him and climbed in the back with the boys. She got them all bundled up under several layers of sleeping bags, as it was getting quite cold without the heater on and they went to sleep. Jason was driving himself nuts thinking about what might be happening to Evan and the women. His strong sense of duty made him feel guilty for staying behind, but he knew Evan was right; his place was with Sarah and the boys.

As the sun began to shine through the tree branches, a glimmer of light caught Jason's eye and startled him awake. He flinched and grabbed his rifle, only to realize that he had simply dozed off during the night. He turned and looked through the sliding glass window that led back into the camper shell to see that his wife and sons were still sound asleep.

He quietly slipped out of the truck so as not to wake them and checked out their surroundings in the daylight. It looked like they were on a power line access road due to the fact that there were some overhead lines leading to a tower, just before the lines went up and over the hill. He couldn't hear any buzzing from the lines, so he figured they were offline too. He carefully walked down the dirt road to find Eight Mile Road. He heard a vehicle approaching and ducked back into the bushes to observe from cover. As it rounded the corner and came into view, he noticed it was a desert tan Humvee. He remained in hiding as it approached. As it came up on his position, which was near the entrance of the dirt road, it began to slow down. His heart skipped a beat thinking of what might happen if it turned and drove up the road toward his family with him not there. As it rolled to a stop, the soldiers inside looked up the road, paused for a moment while having a discussion, and then kept going down Eight Mile Road. "Whew," he said under his breath. He also noticed that it had Ohio National Guard markings so it wasn't as bad as if it was a federal vehicle. He did, however, have weapons and ammunition that were probably frowned upon, by even the state authorities given the situation, especially his undocumented sound suppressor on his Remington. That item was illegal without the documentation on a normal day.

After the Humvee was out of sight, he jogged back up the dirt road to his truck in order to keep a better eye on his family. Somehow, Sarah and the boys managed to sleep rather well and didn't wake up until 9 am. Once everyone was up and about, Jason pulled out his Sterno stove and warmed them up some instant oatmeal and mixed them some instant orange flavored drink for breakfast. They ate it sitting on the tailgate of his truck and enjoyed the relative peace and quiet of their little oasis.

After breakfast, the boys played with some sticks, pretending to sword fight. Jason turned to Sarah and said, "So, how are they doing, especially Michael, after what happened back home?"

"Oh, they are tough like their daddy," she said with a smile. "He seems to be blocking it out. I don't think he has thought a whole lot about it just yet. That's probably the best for now." Jason nodded and began to make them some coffee.

"I'll make the coffee," she said. "You lie down and get some sleep. You look horrible. I'll be right here with your .45 on my side watching out, and if anything at all happens, I will wake you. We've got a long way to go, so you need to get your rest while you can." He took her up on her offer, gave her a hug and climbed up into the camper shell of the truck and went to sleep.

He woke up about 4 pm and flinched at first from what was now a built-in feeling that something bad is just around the corner. He listened intently for a moment and could hear the boys and Sarah talking outside, so he knew everything was still okay. He stretched and yawned, climbed out of the truck and said, "Dang, I can't believe I slept that long."

"You needed it so bad," she said.

"Any word from Evan on the radio?"

"No, nothing yet," she replied.

"Well, I need to get into a position to be able to spot him if he comes down the road but can't use the radio for some reason. I'll take one of the walkie-talkies and head down to the end of the road and hide out in the bushes. If anything goes on back here, or if you hear from him on the CB, give me a shout." He changed into camouflage, insulated hunting pants, and jacket. He figured that in the environment he was in, wearing civilian camouflage would look much less threatening than his tactical gear would, should he encounter some sort of authorities.

Just as he started walking down the road, Sarah called him on the CB and said, "He's on I-275 about to make the turn onto Eight Mile Road."

"Outstanding!" Jason replied. "Is he okay?"

"Yes. He said Peggy and Judith are with him, but they did get Zack. He said he would explain more when they got here."

"Roger that," he replied as he jogged on down to the end of the road. As he saw Sarah's car come around the corner, he stood up and waved his arms to get Evan's attention. Evan flinched at first, not recognizing him at a glance with the change of clothes and from being fatigued from their all night and day event. He quickly realized who it was, though, and he felt a sense of relief to be joined back up with the group. He pulled up alongside Jason, who hopped on the trunk of the car and pounded on it to signal him to go. Evan drove up the dirt road and rounded the corner to see the Jones family and their truck safe and sound.

Sarah ran up to the car to greet Peggy and Judith and immediately noticed that Peggy was grief-stricken. She had little

Zack with her and it looked like he had been crying all night with his mother. She helped them out of the car and took them to the back of the truck to get them cleaned up and to get them some coffee, orange drink, and oatmeal.

Jason and Evan walked off for a moment. Jason looked at Evan and said, "Well... how did it go?"

Evan pulled a handful of empty magazines out of his cargo pocket and said, "I have four rounds left in the mag in the gun and that's it, if that says anything."

"Damn," Jason replied.

"Peggy even fired off a few rounds with your .45 she was carrying. I don't think she hit anything though. It was more of a panic reaction. We need to give her some more intensive training and practice time when we get to the Homefront," he said as he put the magazines back into his pocket. "We got into the state okay. There was a National Guard checkpoint at the river crossing just like Ed said. I used the badge story like we talked and it worked like a charm. We got into a few altercations after that with some city rats before we got to her parents' house, which is where we spent the ammo."

He paused for a second, looked Jason in the eye, and said, "Two days ago, a gang of street thugs broke into her parents' house. They raped and killed her mother, then killed her father. They cleaned out the kitchen of their food and then just left. They had no idea poor little Zack was hiding in the utility closet behind the water heater. He heard the entire horrible thing. He had been hiding in the closet for the past two days without food or water. He was afraid to come out because he didn't know they left or even how much time had passed."

Evan wiped a tear from the corner of his eye and took a moment to regain his composure before continuing. "One of the neighbors down the street told us when they saw the home invasion take place. I can't believe they didn't do anything to help. They just cowered in their own home, allowing it to happen. Then again, not everyone is armed and who would they call? The authorities don't care about crime right now. They are all too busy protecting their turf. Anyway, I couldn't leave Peggy and Judith there. They are with us for the long haul now, I guess. I know it's a tragedy, but it sort of feels like they were supposed to be with us all along, anyway," Evan said as he looked at the ground, kicking a stick around.

"Yeah, I felt the same way," said Jason. "About them belonging with us, that is."

Jason patted Evan on the shoulder and said, "You all get some rest, take a nap, and get something to eat. You need it. Sarah and I will keep an eye on things. Then when you are ready to be up and about, we will hit the road for the Homefront."

"Sounds like a plan to me," Evan said as they walked back toward the truck. Evan reclined the driver's seat of the car and took a nap while Peggy, Judith, and Zack slept in the back of Jason's truck.

At about 10 pm that night, Evan woke up adequately rested and ready to go. He got out of the car and walked over to Jason where he, Sarah, and the boys sat around in lawn chairs, toasting marshmallows over Jason's camp stove. "Marshmallow?" asked Jason as he handed Evan a sharpened stick.

"Absolutely," he said, taking the stick and plopping a marshmallow on it. "I like them burnt to a crisp," he said as he stuck it in the fire and watched it burst into flames and sizzle.

"Well," Jason said, "if you are ready to go we can let Peggy and Zack sleep in the back of the truck while we drive. They've had quite the day, and I don't think they are gonna be in their right mind anytime soon. Judith can ride shotgun for you in the car."

"Sounds good to me," Evan said, biting into his marshmallow and burning his tongue. "This trip from hell needs to end soon," he added.

Sarah explained to Peggy, Judith, and Zack what was going on. They were all anxious to get to Tennessee at this point. They needed some of the uncertainty to end. They had each been through a non-stop, life-altering series of events and were quickly reaching mental fatigue. Peggy and Zack climbed up into the back of the truck, Judith joined Evan in the car, and they hit the road. They traveled all night and began getting close to the Homefront just around sunrise. It had been, compared to their previous experiences, a relatively relaxing night. There were a few tense moments, but they had become quite accustomed to dealing with them and were blessed to be able to keep pressing forward without many real delays.

They were within a few miles of the Homefront, and Evan was getting that same excited, yet worried rapid heartbeat and twisted stomach that Jason had felt when he was nearing home. As they started to turn off of the country road and onto the gravel road that led to the front gate, Jason abandoned his left turn and continued straight. Evan followed to see what the problem was, and as he passed the gravel road, he saw an unfamiliar truck parked sideways, blocking the way. He instantly felt a sinking feeling in his chest. Jason drove on down the road about a half mile and pulled over. Off in the distance they heard gunshots; it sounded like they were coming from the direction of the house.

Chapter 20: War on the Homefront

It had been a sleepless night for the families at the Homefront. The invaders took shots at them all night long. One shot at a time, every few minutes, at a different part of the house. Sometimes hitting the steel shutters, other times the doors, other times the brick itself. Griff believed they were using tactics trying to accomplish two things. One was to wear them down; if they could keep them from resting, they would be able to attack come morning with them exhausted and mentally off their game. The other was that he felt they were probing the house. The attackers had focused so many shots at access points, it was like they were trying to find the soft spot. Luckily for them, the Homefront was a hell of a house and had been reinforced in all the right places. The shots also never came from the same direction twice. This told them that they kept moving to avoid the fifty cal, and it also gave the impression that they were surrounded and trapped inside with no clear route for a retreat.

"With all of Evan's preps, did he think of an escape tunnel per chance?" joked Griff over the walkie-talkie to Molly downstairs.

Before Molly could answer, a rough-sounding man's voice came over the walkie-talkie. "If he had, we would be in there too."

Crap! Griff and Molly thought simultaneously. *They've compromised our channel.* They had just lost their communications if they wanted to keep any OPSEC quiet. "What do you want?" demanded Molly on the radio.

"Everything," the man said.

"We don't have anything of value here," she said.

"Oh, you do," he said. "We know what you've got, and we aren't leaving without it."

Griff looked at Greg and said, "Run downstairs and tell Molly to stay off of the walkie-talkies unless it's an emergency. Tell her just to click the mic four times if she needs you to run downstairs to relay a message back up to me. And while you're down there, find out if she sees anything out there because I think those guys are about to make a move." Greg jumped up and ran downstairs to do as his father asked.

He came back up the stairs just a few minutes later, yelling, "Truck at the gate!"

Griff turned around and shoved the fifty barrel out the shooting port, and as soon as he did, bullets started to ring off of the reinforced shutters. They were trying to suppress his fire while a truck charged the gate. Griff didn't flinch at all while the bullets were bouncing off, just feet from him on the other side of the shutters. He held steady, focused the big fifty's scope, zoomed in on where the engine would be on the truck, and let loose a six hundred and sixty grain, full metal jacket projectile that smashed into the engine block of the truck, disabling it instantly. He quickly re-chambered another round, readjusted his aim, and sprayed the driver's blood and brain matter all over the inside windows of the truck. "That'll take a while to clean up," he said under his breath.

"What?" Greg asked.

"Oh nothing, just mumbling to myself," replied Griff.

Just then, a barrage of bullets struck the shutter where Griff was shooting, and a random bullet found its way through the shooting port. It whizzed by Griff and grazed the top of Greg's head. Greg screamed and dropped to the floor, holding his hands on his head as blood ran down his face. Griff let go of the fifty and turned around and limped over to Greg.

"Let me see it," he said forcefully. He pulled Greg's hands out of the way and saw a deep laceration going all the way down to his skull where the bullet grazed off of his head. He could see the impact point on the wall behind him. "You're fine, you're fine!" Griff said. He clicked his mic four times and Judy came running up the stairs. She almost panicked when she saw all of the blood on Greg's face, but Griff reassured her it would be okay. "Just bandage him up to stop the bleeding for now," Griff said.

Downstairs, Molly heard some rustling and struggling by the

window next to the laundry room. "The Pyracanthas! One of those guys is caught up in it by that window."

Jake looked at her, confused and then she said, "The fire thorns!" She ran across the room, grabbed Jake's VZ58, and yelled, "Watch your sisters!" She shoved the VZ barrel through the glass pane on the inside of the window, breaking through to get the barrel through the shooting port, pointed the gun down toward the bush, and emptied the thirty-round magazine into the man. It was the first time she had shot someone and was so caught up in the adrenalin rush, that without a clear view of the assailant, she just shot until it ran dry.

She pulled the gun back in and had just begun to run back to the main basement room, when a man rammed the door with a makeshift battering ram in front of her and in between her and the kids. The structural reinforcements, however, kept the door on its hinges for now. It was just then she realized she had emptied the gun and didn't bring a spare magazine. Jake ran across the room in front of her with the Mossberg 590 in hand and shoved it through the cat door that they had installed for a prone shooting port at the bottom of the door, and blew the man's leg apart. He pulled the shotgun back in, racked a round in the chamber, shoved it back out the hole, and blindly fired another round, killing the man who was now lying right in front of the blast.

Molly ran by him, grabbed him by the arm, and pulled him back into the center basement room. She slammed and locked the security door behind them where they met Judy as she was running back down the stairs. Judy and Molly updated each other on what they had each just seen and done.

Judy said, "Griff thinks they've figured out the fifty can't get a line on them once they are in close to the house, so if they draw the fifty's fire up front, they rush the house from the rear, or possibly vice versa. Either way, these guys are coordinating their attacks."

Out on the road, Evan and Jason quickly developed a plan. They left the women and children with the truck and put several cans of ammo and Jason's Remington in the car. Evan looked at Jason and said, "I don't have enough 5.56mm left to get into a fight. In hindsight, we should have hiked up on that hill and stripped those guys you smoked at that roadside ambush of their gear. But hey, we are new to the whole end of the world thing and hindsight is 20/20. Give me one of your SKSs and a can of ammo and a bunch of mags."

Jason ran back to the truck and grabbed two of the SKSs. He slung one over his back and tossed the other one to Evan. Both had been fitted with thirty-round magazines and he tossed Evan a magazine bag containing eight loaded mags. He also grabbed an SKS for himself, as well, to back up the slow rate of fire from the Remington bolt action. They then jumped into the car and took off toward the gravel road.

Evan said, "You remember the tree stands, right?"

"Sure do," replied Jason.

"Well, I'm giving you your hunting license. Go from stand to stand with your Remington and snipe at those guys. They will never think to look up into the trees, and if they do, remember you can rappel down, using the tree for cover. There is a climbing rig in each stand. I'm gonna try and be a thorn in their side, distracting them while you take them out. Just don't shoot me from a distance because you can't tell who I am."

"No promises," said Jason as he took off into the woods with his Remington in his hands and his SKS on his back.

Evan also slipped off into the woods, but he took a different course and set out to flank the truck that was parked sideways to block the road. He crept up on the lone gunman they had left behind to watch the truck. *He must be their rookie*, Evan thought as he stalked the man like he was a game animal. Evan readied the SKS with his right hand, and then picked up a rock and tossed it at the side of the truck with his left. The man heard the metallic thud as the rock hit the truck. He spun around in the direction of the noise as Evan lit him up from the side, sending three thirty-caliber bullets into his vitals. The man dropped dead to the ground before he even knew where Evan was.

After Evan had verified that the scene was secure and it did not appear anyone was coming back to check on their cohort, he snuck over to the truck and opened the gas cap. He reached down and tore off a piece of his own undershirt from underneath his jacket. He twisted it up, shoved the t-shirt down into the gas cap, and lit it with the survival lighter that he always carried in his jacket. Once it was burning, he jogged on down the road toward the house and ducked back into the woods.

Meanwhile, Jason had come to his first tree stand. He climbed up the small tree stand hunting ladder that consisted of strap on climbing sticks. It was hardly noticeable at a glance, keeping the location of the stand hidden. Once he got up in the tree, he strapped himself into the harness for a quick egress. He raised his Remy up, propped it on a tree branch, and started scanning through his scope for an opportunity. From his vantage point, he had a great view of the field of fire in the front of the house. Just then, he heard an explosion coming from back on the road.

The explosion Jason heard was the car fire that Evan made out of the aggressor's pickup truck. He did it to get the attention of the aggressors and to help create a diversion for Jason or anyone at the house who may need a moment to get a shot off. Just then, Evan saw a rough-looking man in his early thirties, with a tattoo wrapping all the way around his neck and up the side of his face, running down the road to investigate the explosion. Evan waited until the man jogged just past his hiding spot, and he let two rounds go from the SKS. The first shot struck the man in the lower back and the second the back of his head, spilling his brains all over the road.

From Jason's vantage point, the man who ran back into Evan's trap gave away a hunkered down position where he and two other men lay low. They were using their position to occasionally spray a harassing fire at the house. Jason didn't know it at the time, but that fire was directed at Griff to keep him occupied with the fifty out front while their cohorts approached the house from the rear. Jason zoomed in his scope to its maximum zoom and scanned for a target of opportunity. It was at least two hundred yards away, but with the powerful Nightforce scope, Jason was able to make out the top of a bald man's head. He adjusted his shot for the prevailing wind and let it fly. The impact of the round took the very top of the man's head off, spraying matter all over the man sitting next to him. This caused the second man to move, giving away his position as well. Jason chambered another round and shot through some thin brush that was blocking his view to where he assumed the man would be. The bullet ripped right through the man's side. The impact of the bullet tossed the body slightly into view, just enough that Jason knew he got the kill. He then patiently watched for any more movement from the position. He didn't see anything after a few minutes, so he slung the rifle on his back and rappelled down the tree. He then took off running through the woods to the next tree stand location.

Griff watched the position that Jason had just decimated through the scope on the fifty. He couldn't get a shot at the guys from where he was, but he could see the crossfire coming from ninety degrees to his position taking the men out. Griff got on the radio and said, "The cavalry is here, dirtbags. You picked the wrong house today." He wasn't sure who was doing the shooting, but he thought a little psychological warfare couldn't hurt. Molly heard this and thought to herself, *Is that them? Are they finally here? Oh, God, please let it be.*

Evan ducked back into the woods and circled around the house to the right while Jason's position took him around to the left. Jason reached the next tree stand, climbed up, got himself set up quickly and was back to searching for a target. He could now get a clear view of the left side of the house as well as most of the back. He scanned the area with his scope and saw the two bodies behind the house that Molly and Jake had dispatched a little while earlier. He kept scanning the area until he saw two men behind the stacked firewood. The firewood was almost around the other side of the house in the back. Jason knew if he tried but missed and they ran, they would likely go around toward Evan. He picked up his walkie-talkie and said, "Ev, sending."

Evan heard the transmission and thought to himself, *I hope that means what I think it does.* He crept up to the edge of the woods on the right front side of the house and held his aim on the back corner. Jason took aim at the clearest target he could get, which was one of the men's boots, from what appeared to be him having his foot out behind himself while in a kneeling position. Jason carefully took his aim and squeezed the trigger. Through the scope, he could see the .300 Win Mag round rip through the man's boot, shattering his foot and blowing parts of it out the other side. The man fell backward in agony and Jason quickly chambered another round and ended his misery with a shot center mass. The man next to him, realizing that they were being fired upon from an unknown position behind them, retreated from the wood pile, running directly towards where Evan patiently waited. The man ran right into Evan's sights as Evan put three rounds into him, dropping him like a sack of potatoes.

Griff watched through his scope and saw Evan dart out of the woods after his muzzle flashes gave his position away. "Holy crap, I think that's Evan!" he said out loud.

Evan crept up to the corner of the house and lay down in the prone position, being careful not to get into the Pyracantha bushes while using them as visual cover. Jason could now see him through his scope from his elevated position. He then turned to scan the rest of the yard, where he saw a man hiding in the chicken coop. Jason got on the walkie-talkie and made a chicken sound, *"Bock, bock, bacock."*

Evan, again hoping he understood Jason's message, placed his sights on the chicken coop. Jason topped off his Remington, took aim at the coop roughly where the man was hiding, and started a relentless pounding on the shack. Shot after shot after shot, the air around the coop was filled with feathers and flying wood debris. Finally, knowing he was not going to be able to hold out there any longer, the man bolted out of the coop. Just as Jason was about to pull the trigger to again fire on the coop, he saw him make a run for it. He adjusted his aim and sent a round into his back. At exactly the same time, Evan saw him break cover and begin to run; he also put several rounds into the man and he was torn to shreds from both sides in an instant.

When the man's body hit the ground, Evan and Jason both just lay in wait, scanning the area, watching for any signs of movement. They waited patiently for a little over a half hour before Jason got back on the walkie-talkie and said, "I think we got the whole herd."

Evan responded, "Yep, I think so. Don't shoot me. I'm breaking cover." He then yelled, "Molly! Are you in there?"

"Yes, yes, yes, oh my God, yes! Thank God you are here!" said Molly in a frantic, yet elated voice.

"Tell everyone in the house to hold their fire. Jason is going to cover me while I sweep the area to make sure it's clear," he responded.

For the next twenty minutes, Evan carefully and patiently swept the perimeter of the house. He went in and out of the woods, all while Jason covered him from the stand. He counted eight bodies total. He yelled from the front yard to Griff upstairs, "How many were there?"

"Not sure, couldn't see them all from here," Griff replied.

Evan picked up his walkie-talkie and said, "Jason, what do you think?"

"Looks clear to me and I've got the best view in the place. I think we are good," said Jason over the radio.

"Okay, then, I'm going in the house. You get out of that tree and go get your family and the rest. I'll have the front gate unlocked by the time you get back."

"Roger Roger!" he replied.

Evan walked around to the back door, stepping over the two dead bodies. He rang the doorbell and said, "Hi, Honey, I'm home."

Molly opened the door, grabbed Evan, pulled him inside, and collapsed on the floor with him while holding him tightly as she broke down into tears. Jake, carrying Sammy and Lilly, came running from behind as they were yelling, "Daddy, Daddy, Daddy!" and they all joined in on one big group hug.

Griff came limping down the stairs, exhausted and fatigued, looked at Evan, smiled, and said, "I think we are even on the beer."

"Yeah, well, heal yourself up quick. We are going to have a lot of work to do around here."

The End

The New Homefront Series is continued in - *The Guardians: The New Homefront, Volume 2.*

A Note from the Author

First and foremost, I want to thank you for purchasing and reading this book. It has been a labor of love and an amazing experience for me to be able to put my heart and soul into a story that hopefully entertained and informed you. This story will be continued with new books coming out from Homefront Books in *The New Homefront* series.

I also want to thank Jason D. Jean, a good friend, who contributed his time and effort in helping me with this project. His knowledge and insight on many of the subjects contained in this book were key in the development of the story and the finished product of the book.

In addition to being a freelance author, I currently work full time as a Captain for a large domestic, regional airline. I served over twenty years in the U.S. Navy/U.S. Navy Reserve and retired as a Chief Petty Officer. In addition, I have both military and federal law enforcement experience. I am married with three children, and in my spare time I am an amateur competitive shooter and an avid hunter and outdoorsman. My wife and I share an interest in homesteading and self-sufficiency and apply those interests to our daily lives on our property in East Tennessee.

Visit

www.homefrontbooks.com
www.facebook.com/homefrontbooks

or follow on Twitter @stevencbird for information and updates on the upcoming books to be released as part of the series. The sequel to *The Last Layover* is *The Guardians: The New Homefront,*

Volume 2, which is available now, as well as *The Blue Ridge Resistance: The New Homefront, Volume 3*, and *The Resolution: The New Homefront, Volume 4*.

Thank you very much, and I hope you return to read more of my books in the future.

Respectfully,

Steven C. Bird

42938315R00123

Made in the USA
Lexington, KY
11 July 2015